for [illegible] ("Bill")
looking
her vision of
King of Shadows —
a minor, but often
entertaining work

lots of

Love

Adina
Saratoga 2003

Peace

BEFORE HE WAS FAMOUS

The Medieval Mystery Plays were dramatized stories from the Bible, performed by ordinary working men who belonged to the local trades guilds, usually at the Feast of Corpus Christi, in early summer. After King Henry VIII broke away from the Church of Rome, the new Protestant authorities abolished Corpus Christi and gradually the plays died out. One of the last performances we know about was at Coventry in 1580, the year in which this book is set, but people have always enjoyed acting. There is no reason to suppose that they did not go on staging their own plays, for the fun of it.

Shakespeare was a professional actor and a professional writer. The London theatre company he belonged to was highly successful, but when he wrote *A Midsummer Night's Dream* he seems to have been remembering a different kind of acting, and a very different kind of company.

Also by Jan Mark

Heathrow Nights

Other titles in Signature

Skellig
David Almond

Scorched
Josephine Poole

Mondays are Red
Nicola Morgan

Escape
Foundling
Undercurrents
Smoke Trail
June Oldham

STRATFORD BOYS

Jan Mark

Hodder
Children's
Books

A division of Hodder Headline Limited

For Chris Kloet

A Catalogue record for this book is available from the British Library

ISBN 0 340 86097 9

Typeset in Bembo by Avon DataSet Ltd,
Bidford-on-Avon, Warwickshire

Printed and bound in Great Britain by
Clays Ltd, St Ives PLC, Bungay, Suffolk

The paper and board used in this paperback are natural
recyclable products made from wood grown in sustainable forests.
The manufacturing processes conform to the environmental
regulations of the country of origin.

Hodder Children's Books
a division of Hodder Headline Limited
338 Euston Road
London NW1 3BH

One

The Shakespeares had the builders in again. As Adrian Croft crossed into Henley Street he saw Wat Lambert's ladder propped against the front entrance, and a tell-tale haze hung about the doorway. Going down the passage between the hall and the workshop he plunged into a dense fog of dust where a section of the plaster had cracked and fallen away from the new door frame. Dick was crouched over a heap which he had swept together with his hands, patting it into a smooth mound. He poked a hole in it with his finger and aimed a mouthful of spit that he had been working up in readiness.

'It won't come again,' Wat the plasterer said.

'Come where?'

'That old plaster, that's dead. You can't mix it up twice.'

'Why not?' William, the eldest brother, stuck his head through the doorway like a bullock gazing from its byre.

'Because.' Wat glared at him through the dust. 'Here you are again, asking questions. I've got work to do if you haven't.'

'I'm interested, that's all. I just wondered—'

'You've got your trade, I've got mine. Your old dad would have something to say if I came into the shop, poking around, asking you how to cut gloves. You aiming to do this work yourself and cheat an honest workman?'

'You'd have told Dick all about it if I hadn't come in.'

'How old is he, six? He's not going to run off with trade secrets.' Wat turned and saw Adrian hovering in the passage. 'Oh God, here's another one. What are you after, eavesdropping on honest workmen?'

'Your secrets are safe with me, Wat. I came to see him,' Adrian said, nodding towards Will. 'I didn't want to get in your way.'

'Well, you are in it. One of you shift your carcase, in or out.'

Wat stood back from the doorway, swinging his arms to fan them through, one way or the other. Will stepped out, pausing a fraction too long to look at the fresh plaster.

'You won't learn nothing by looking,' Wat said. 'This isn't a book.'

'But it is to you, Wat,' Will said, riskily. 'You can read that plaster as I read words.'

'Is that a riddle?' Wat's cropped hair seemed to be rising in a crest like the hackles of an enraged dog. Adrian shoved his friend towards the street door.

Will never knew when to stop. 'But you see as much in that wall as I see in printed words. As you said, your trade—'

'If I'm so learned, reading walls, how come I'm a plasterer and not a schoolman? Bugger off.' Wat's voice followed them down the passage. 'If I go and stand in the church and read the wall will they make me Parson?'

'That didn't do much to mend matters,' Adrian said as they came out into the street. 'He thinks you were making game of him.'

'By asking questions?'

'By telling him your book-learning was no cleverer than his wall-learning. He's not that stupid.'

'It was a manner of speaking. What's the harm in knowing how the plaster works?' Will complained. 'If he told me, I still wouldn't know how to use it.'

'Think what he said about the gloves. All tradesmen are jealous. You should know, you're always asking people about their trades and crafts. They never tell you.'

'Wat's hardly a master craftsman. I don't suppose he knows why the plaster comes hard after he spreads it, he just knows it does.' They were sauntering down Bridge Street now, towards the river, the shadows lengthening around them. 'Why did you fetch me out?' Will said.

'I didn't mean to. If Wat hadn't been there, wouldn't you have fetched me in? I thought you'd still be working.'

'All orders are made up, and Father's cautious about having too much stock in hand. He's keeping the best skins aside in case we get called on to supply a wedding and have nothing suitable laid by.'

'And nothing to pay for new skins with?' This was not a diplomatic remark. Adrian's father was in much the same situation, most local tradesmen were, but Robert Croft did not have a wife and four children to feed, with another on the way.

'You know how it goes at the moment,' Will said. 'When times are hard people find they don't need new clothes as much as they thought they did.'

'Your father's not been to a council meeting for a while, has he?'

John Shakespeare had not been to church for a while, either. Will squinnied sidelong at Adrian. 'What's that got to do with new clothes? Did your father send you with a message for him, then?'

'Not a message, exactly. But at the last meeting they were talking about what the town might do for a Whitsun pastime.'

Will finally looked alert. 'Are we to have players?'

'I don't think so. I've not heard that any of the big companies are coming our way this spring.'

'I'd never wish a plague on London,' Will said, 'but it does drive them out. Would we ever see plays done in Stratford if the plague didn't close the London playhouses?'

'You've not done so badly. Coventry, Kenilworth . . .'

'You make it sound as if I went every year. The Queen may never come to Kenilworth again and if what they say is true there'll be no more Corpus Christi plays in Coventry – or anywhere else.'

'Since there's no more Corpus Christi, probably not,' Adrian said. 'And the London companies don't come here unless they have to. That's why the council was discussing a Whitsun pastime.'

'Or the lack of it.'

'They're worried. Trade's bad, money's short. People need their hearts lifted. If there's no travelling company coming our way, can't we put on something ourselves?'

'Put on what? A play?' They were passing the Bear. 'Do you have tuppence about you?'

The inn was fairly empty at that hour, most men being still at work or at their dinners. Will sat on a bench by the window. Adrian stood treat.

'What has this to do with Father?' Will said.

'I thought he was always in the mood for a play.'

'He's not in the mood for anything just now,' Will said. 'He can't read the order book but he can see when there's nothing in it.'

'Hard times won't last for ever. Trade always picks up in spring – I heard a cuckoo this morning,' Adrian said. 'Perhaps the thought of Whitsun revels will cheer him. He didn't drag himself over to Kenilworth that time so that you could tell us all about it. My father says that he was ever the first to move that the council should license a company. And, didn't you tell me once . . . he has a playbook?'

'Somewhere about the place. I've never seen it. Anyway, you need more than a playbook to put on a play; players, for a start; costumes, properties. Remember Essex's Men last summer? One of their robes would have fetched enough to feed our poor for a year.'

'If we put on our own play,' Adrian said, 'no one would expect us to be got up like my Lord of Essex's Men.'

'Are you in earnest?' Will said. 'The council thinks we should put on our own play? *Us?*'

'I don't think that's quite what they had in mind – but why not? You, me, Anthony, Philip . . . we've all learned acting in school.'

'Speaking the old Roman poets with gestures. Terence, Plautus . . . imagine how that will go down with someone like Wat. And most of the audience will be just like Wat.'

'So? When the travelling companies come, Wat and his friends are right there, enjoying themselves, even if they don't follow more than one word in five. They know love and sorrow and betrayal and death. Everyone enjoys a slaying if it's well done, with plenty of blood.'

'Am I following you?' Will said. 'The council wants a

play put on for Whitsun and your father thinks my father is going to bring it about?'

'My father thought your father might advise—'

'Why doesn't he ask him, then?'

'When was he last at a council meeting? Who minds the stall on Market Days?'

'I do.'

'Yes, yes, *I* know that. Father thought if I asked you, you might mention it to him. You might just ask to see that playbook.'

John Shakespeare could not read but he could reckon figures in his head. He was doing it now as they sat around the fire after supper, irritably batting his hand at various children when they broke into his calculations with daft questions.

When he had had the chimney put in, two years ago, so that a floor could be installed to create upstairs rooms, he had not foreseen the disruption; first the chimney stack, the hearth, new rafters, walls; then the staircase, a nightmare of dust; mortar, plaster, brickdust, sawdust, builders apparently encamped on the premises. And the escalating cost, just when trade was at its worst for years. He had told his wife it would be worth it, after seeing cosy firesides in other men's houses, but as soon as two or more Shakespeares were gathered together a row was bound to break out.

'The playbook?' he snapped, finally answering Will, the last to ask a daft question. 'What do you want with the playbook?'

Will wondered whether to tell him straight and court an outburst – which would be justified, he thought, at the roundabout way in which he had been approached by Robert Croft. Still, the old man was not particularly approachable at the moment, which was why he and Adrian had got the job.

'We were talking of a pastime at Whitsun,' Will said. 'Perhaps a play—'

'We?'

'Adrian Croft and I.'

'Are you on the council now?'

'No, Father. But if there's no travelling company coming we thought . . . we might put on a play ourselves.'

'You and Robert Croft's boy? What the devil do you know about putting on plays?'

'Not a thing,' Will said, 'but that's no less than anyone else. And you told me once about the playbook – that's *more* than anyone else has.'

'I don't know where it is.'

'Do you know where it isn't?'

'Mind your tongue,' Will's mother said, tiredly. She was nearing her time, great-bellied and awkward in her chair on the far side of the hearth.

'I only meant, if we were to look for it there are places it couldn't be.' His father continued to scowl. Will tried to lighten the atmosphere. 'In the dough trough, for instance. In the cheese wring.'

'In the pork barrel,' Dick piped up.

'Will you be quiet!' John roared.

Dick subsided, biting his lip. 'I thought we were playing a game.'

'We are not playing a game. Your brother is making a fool of himself as usual,' John said, unfairly. 'Go to your bed. How often must you be told?

'You didn't tell—'

'Go on, Dick,' Will said, before his little brother could spark the explosion that he himself had feared to set in train.

Dick had not yet learned to read the danger signs, had never needed to. The indulged baby, doubly precious since Anne died last year, was about to lose his place if their mother were to be safely delivered in May. Being the youngest had sheltered him from Father's deteriorating temper over the last year or so, but now he was feeling, for the first time, the unkind breath of reality at his back, pitched out of Mammy's lap by the child to come, into the chilly substitute of the petty school. He bowed to his father, kissed his mother goodnight and went drooping to the door. Will caught Joan's eye and she followed him out to administer comfort and consolation, the only sister living now and fast learning to be a buffer between Father and the three boys. If Gilbert left school and joined them in the shop they would all be constantly under one another's feet.

Father sat glaring at the fire. Mother's eyes were closed. Gilbert crouched at the window overlooking the street, to catch the last of the light as he studied his lesson for tomorrow. He took care to stay out of family rows, never knowing whose side to take.

Will got up quietly and slipped out, meaning to leave the house, but as he went down the passage he heard his father's voice from the doorway behind him.

'Wait, Son . . .' The gunpowder train had burned out after all. There would be no explosion. He turned.

'It would be good to have a play at Whitsun. But what makes you think you can handle it?'

'I didn't think so, Father. Perhaps Master Cottam at the school might take it on?'

'If he's doing his job properly, he won't have time. Well, well, let's find the playbook. It's in the shop, in the cupboard with the patterns, though it's a few years since I looked at it. Not having the need . . .'

Father's respect for book-learning came from his having had none himself. He liked to handle the volumes that William borrowed and brought home, looking reverently at the printed pages that he could no more read than could Wat the plasterer, only Wat regarded literacy as a secret society that excluded him by communicating in signs and marks that made no sense to honest men.

They went into the deserted workshop. On the eastern side of the house it benefitted from morning light, but now stood cold and shadowed. John Shakespeare unlocked the pattern cupboard, reached in and located the thing he was searching for by touch. Will looked out of the window to where a last fugitive ray of sunlight slid across the flags of the garden, under shrubs, round the legs of the bench beneath the elm.

'It's a Corpus Christi play, Son,' John said. 'I had it from a man of the north country a long time since. The way he told it, the plays were as good as the ones at Coventry, three days it took to put them all on, from the *Fall of Lucifer* to *Judgement Day*. All that changed when Queen Mary died; the plays had to be mended to please the churchmen. They'd call in the playbooks, meddling and changing, and the guildsmen would have to learn them all anew. But they did, for how could they go to the people and say, "No plays this year, we can't learn them in time, they being so chopped about." Then one year they were kept back so long that there was no time to do anything about it.'

'What happened?'

'Nothing happened.' John looked over his shoulder as if there might be unseen listeners lurking in the shadows

11

under the work benches. 'It was a base, underhand business. They never said outright, "No more plays; plays are forbidden at Corpus Christi now." They let the guildsmen take the blame for it. You don't repeat that outside this room, you understand. For all I know, that's what's happened at Coventry.'

He closed the cupboard and turned. There was enough light to see what he held, not the book with covers that Will had been loosely imagining, but a few ragged sheets, stitched together; not printed but hand written. He could see that much before the sun went down and the last of the light leached out of the garden.

'Who was he, the man who gave you this?'

'I never knew more of his name but Thomas. He was travelling south, I met him at the Bay Tree in Banbury. He was old and taken sick in the night and he wanted a priest – he was of the old faith. He knew I was a glover, so was he, we'd had some talk at supper. I sat with him till he died. I was a stranger there, where was I to find a priest? Who dare I ask? He gave me this – I'd told him that we still had plays here in the middle lands, as we did, then. Perhaps he wanted to think it would live on after him. It's the Glovers' Play of his town.'

'Which town?'

'I forget, it was a good ten years back. Not one I knew the name of or I'd have it still, but as I recall, this is *The Slaying of Abel*.'

Will took the booklet into his hands. It was too dark to see what was written on the pages but – ten years. It was in poor condition; not so much ragged, his fingers told him, as gnawed.

'Father, are your patterns safe? I think there must be mice in that cupboard.'

The play was forgotten. 'Bring a light! Fetch Malkin. I'll clear the shelves.'

Will pushed the playbook into his coat front and went back to the hall. 'Gilbert, bring a candle to the shop!' He swept up the dozing cat from the hearth and bore her before him. 'Do your duty, Malkin.'

'The worst of it is,' Will said, dangling the playbook in front of Adrian, 'half of it's missing.'

'Which half?' They were sitting with Adrian's cousin Hugh in the churchyard after evensong, at the eastern end, nearest to the river. Round at the side people were dancing to Jakey Grafton's bagpipe. The bulk of the building muffled the whoops and catcalls, but the bagpipe keened persistently, like wind in a chimney.

'Mice have been at every page and the last three are altogether gone.'

'That's not so bad,' Adrian said. 'At least we know how it ends. It's not as though we have to guess what will happen.'

'We know how it ends in the Bible.'

'Won't this be the same? There is only one story of Cain and Abel.'

'I don't think so. I mean, yes, there is only one story, but there are ways of telling it. When I saw it done in Coventry, Cain had a servant. There is no servant in the book of Genesis – and no wives, neither.'

'Who said anything about wives?'

'In this play, Cain has a wife.'

'Cain did have a wife,' Hugh butted in. 'The Scriptures tell us so. ". . . and she conceived and bare Enoch and he builded a city." '

'Yes, yes, I know. Don't you remember at school, we asked the usher where Cain's wife came from since there was no one else alive on earth but Adam and Eve, and were beaten for it. But this is different, look. Cain has a wife *before* he kills Abel, and so does Abel, too.'

The play was written in English, a clear firm hand, although many of the words, being from the north, were strange to them, but here and there were lines of Latin, to direct the players. Adrian looked where Will's finger was pointing: *Enter Uxor Abel.*

'Was that proper,' Hugh said, 'to make up people who never lived?'

Adrian was already regretting his invitation to Hugh to join them. Hugh knew Holy Writ to the letter and used it like a plumbline, everything else measured against it.

'How do we know they never lived? If Cain had a wife, why not Abel? They were grown men.'

'The Scriptures do not say that Abel had a wife.' Hugh did not give up easily.

'The Scriptures do not say that Cain had a servant, but whoever wrote the play at Coventry thought he *probably* had a servant or a workman, so he made one up. So did this northcountryman. Anyway, there are not many persons in the story of Cain and Abel. Cain has to have someone to talk to, otherwise he'd just stand there shouting, "I'm sinful! I'm corrupted!" '

'But then the playwright is being as God, creating people. If God did not create a wife for Abel and the Scriptures do not tell us that he had a wife, isn't it blasphemy for the playwright to create her instead?'

'It doesn't work like that!' Will shouted. 'You read the old Roman plays at school – and acted them too, didn't you? And did you stand there arguing with the Master about whether God or Seneca created Hercules?'

'Aye, but they were heathens,' Hugh said.

'If we put on this play you had better speak the part of God,' Will said. 'You seem to share His way of thinking.'

'How can we put it on at all if it isn't all there – by Christ, I wish Jakey would get a cough of the lungs and stop his wind for ever.' Adrian did not love the bagpipe.

'They'll all go home when it's dark. As you said, we know what happens. We can work out what's missing,' Will said.

'You can work it out. I've no skill at playwriting.'

'No more have I.'

'You write poetry.'

'This is not poetry. It's in verse, but it's plain men speaking plain English – well, most of it's plain.'

Adrian pounced. 'Then you won't have any trouble with it, will you? Think on it; Abel's wife is missing and the mice have been at Mistress Cain, but she's as bad as he is. He bawls at her, she berates him, he beats her with a threshing flail, she throws turnips. It's an ill marriage. Abel and his wife will be quite the other way about, the type of all that's good and seemly – so no problem there. When God tells Cain that his brother's blood crieth to him from the ground, very likely Abel's wife wails and rends her garments.'

'The mice have eaten most of God, too,' Will said.

Two

The most significant thing Will had learned from his attempts at poetry was that there were very few words that rhymed with love: dove, above, shove and, of course, glove; and possibly move, at a pinch. His trial run at a sonnet about a glover in love had come to grief on the fifth line. What remained of *The Slaying of Abel* was in rhyming couplets. Unless he began all over again he would have to stick with it as it was. What could he do with it? The whole story was over in a few verses in the book of Genesis; so no clues there.

Will did not take the playbook into the shop during hours. To be seen reading when he ought to be at work would not impress Stephen, his fellow apprentice, still less Martin, the journeyman glover. In any case, he had the whole thing in his head, now. He was working on fancy belts at the moment, straightforward stitching which left his mind free to worry at the play.

Cain struck him as an early version of Wat Lambert the plasterer, although he knew that this was unjust. Wat was crabbed and surly, but only to people he considered to be in danger of getting above themselves. With his mates in the Bear he was affable enough and he never lingered there tippling when he ought to have been working. Cain, on the other hand, railed and ranted, insulted his servant, his brother and his Creator, knocked his wife about and finally committed fratricide. Why hadn't God struck him dead? Good men had died for less in other parts of the Bible.

But Cain had to live. After Abel's death Eve had borne a third son, Seth; but Seth's line had died out. From Cain was descended Noah, the one good man left on earth who had built the Ark and saved his family. That was careful forethought on God's part. Now, the play of *Noah's Flood* was good sport, with nine speaking parts. Whoever had written the Glovers' Play had been frustrated by the shortage of persons, having only Cain, Abel and God, and had hit upon the idea of wives. At least he had not given God a wife.

'Chicken skin!'

His father was in the doorway, ready, as usual, to explode, but this time it seemed as much with laughter as anger. 'Will, do we have a chicken skin about the place? I should have told him to take himself to the chicken skinners.'

'Is this an order, Father?'

'Oh, yes, a wedding at Ascensiontide; one-and-ninety pairs of gloves, dogskin, cheveril and – and—'

18

'Chicken skin. Can it be done?'

'Seemingly. Peter Starling, marrying Mary Horn, has a fancy to give her as a token a pair of chicken-skin gloves in a walnut.'

'Did he say why? He can't have come up with the idea by himself.'

'Oh, he heard of it from a man who had it from another who had it from a lady at Court, that a lover gave his mistress a walnut, and when she opened it there were these Goddam chicken-skin gloves inside. Only chicken skin would roll up small enough. Now this young Starling wants to surprise his Mary with a pair.'

Will was already making calculations. 'We'll need two hens, Father. The gloves must be long in the gauntlet, that'll be the neck. Then there'll be no need for side seams. Cut one glove whole from each skin and run a single seam from the tip of the thumb, up and down each finger. It will have to be fine sewing – perhaps there might be a third hen to practise on.'

'How in hell's name are we going to flay and tan hens? Who's got hens to spare? Are we eating chicken's flesh today? Am I to go around town begging for hens? I'm a whittawer. I prepare white leather. I don't do chicken skins.'

'Did you quote Master Starling a price?'

'Of course.'

19

'For the gloves or for the hens? This is to be a special gift, he must expect to pay for it. If the gloves were to be cheveril you would charge him for the leather and the labour. If they were to be perfumed you would charge him for the essence. If he wants chicken-skin gloves he must pay for the hens too. We can't buy the skins without hens in them.'

'You'll be a businessman yet, Will,' his father said, with grudging respect.

'Or let him supply the hens. You can advise him on the finest quality hide.'

'What is the finest quality hide?'

'A hen's a hen. You might pull out a few feathers, suck your teeth as masons do when they see another man's work, and say, "This is poor skin" or "This makes a sow's hide feel like silk". You may have some sport with this, Father, but be quick. We don't know how long it takes to cure a chicken skin. And it's the wrong time of year for walnuts. If Mother's laid none by we'll have to go searching.'

It was pleasing to see the old man so pleased, but it had been inspiration rather than craftsmanship that had revealed to Will how a chicken's neck, with the head off, would make a perfect gauntlet.

'He might as well have asked for frog skins,' John said, going out again. Martin and Stephen allowed themselves to laugh once the door had closed. Will, looking out of the window a few minutes later, saw his father in the garden gazing thoughtfully over the fence into the hen run. Joan was collecting eggs. Father was pointing, Joan explaining.

She had names for all the hens, and the cockerel – Sir Solomon, because he had many wives. Will could see that she was gratified by Father's interest; she did not know the reason for it. Martha, Molly, Dorcas, Deborah and their sisters might all be eaten when their time came, but to cut them off early for the sole purpose of experimenting with their skins . . . ?

Frogs might, in fact, be easier to work with. Left to themselves they seemed to become leather by nature after death. A matched pair could supply gloves for a fairy; little hands, no bigger than a hare's foot, or an ape's. Apes had hands like a man, he had heard. He had never seen one.

For all he knew, there were no such things as apes. How could a man trust everything that he was taught unless he saw for himself? He had never seen a fairy, either, or a ghost. Many had. As children they had hung around outside the charnel house by the church, thrilled and terrified by the thought of the bones stacked inside, the mirthless grins and sightless eye sockets of skulls, and scared themselves silly with tales of imagined phantoms and walking skeletons. Could these dry bones live? Oh yes, most assuredly.

Back at the bench he picked up the belt again. As he resumed work the chicken-skin gloves were forgotten and the lines of the play began to run through his head as if he were stitching them.

How if Abel's ghost should walk on at the end of the play and follow Cain into exile, into the land of Nod? That would be a great effect; well done it could freeze the marrow. But would it be blasphemy? Adrian's glum cousin Hugh would think so. Hugh feared that it might be blasphemous to create people in any case; he would disapprove even more of a ghost. Since the puritans — and Hugh was certainly shaping up to be a puritan — had discovered that the English Bible contained no reference to purgatory and summarily abolished it, a dim view was taken of the idea that spirits might walk the earth. Either they were damned in hell or blissful in heaven. But the image of a pallid figure, trailing blood-boltered cerecloths, had a certain charm, especially if it should speak, doomfully, and Cain fled before it.

It would not make a great deal of sense, Biblically, since Cain, in the end, seemed to have done all right for himself. But what a way to finish! If only they weren't hamstrung by having to abide by Holy Writ, with gloomy Hugh shooting down every bright idea as it took wing.

But then, Will thought, *did* they need to be? What time and the mice had left of the Glovers' Play could

22

never be put on as it was. If they used it he would have to furnish at least the half that was missing; why not the other half as well? It was a fine story, it did not have to be about Cain and Abel at all. God need never come into it in which case they would not have to worry about offending Him. Two brothers, a shepherd and a farmer, one meek and gentle, the other a brawling braggart . . . and it need not rhyme, he could use iambic pentameters, blank verse.

'Call that stitching?' Martin barked in his ear. 'Pull it all out and start again.'

The Bear was riotous this evening. A close-fought game of shove-groat was nearing its climax and the crowd around the shovelboard, said to be the longest in Warwickshire, was bellowing encouragement. At the other end of the room Will could scarcely make himself heard above the din.

'. . . the other brother's a brawling braggart who beats his wife and his servants, rails against his father and kills his brother in a fit of envy.'

'Kills his mother?' Hugh shouted.

'Kills his *brother*!'

'Keep your voices down,' Adrian said. 'You talk so loud of murder and we'll have the constables in.' He looked round nervously but no one was paying them any attention – yet.

'We know he kills his brother,' Hugh said. 'It is in Holy Writ.'

'Ah, no. This is not about Cain and Abel. It's – it's – Cadmus and Arcturus, two Roman kinsmen.'

The shovelboard mob erupted. Somebody had won. There were loud demands for ale all round, loser to pay.

'I thought you were going to patch the play, not write a new one,' Adrian said, as the racket subsided. 'Is there time?'

'Nearly six weeks to Whitsun.'

'We have to rehearse. We haven't a company to play it, yet. How long will it take you to write it?'

'Oh, not so very long,' Will said, with an airy confidence that Adrian did not share. 'After all, I have the hardest part done already, that's the plot. And the main roles – the brothers, the father. All I have to do is write what they say.'

'That's the easy part, is it?' Hugh said.

'It is for me, but don't expect me to do anything else at the same time. I've enough to keep me busy in the shop – we have to discover how to make chicken-skin gloves before Ascensiontide. No, there's more to a play than the writing of it. When I've done, you and Gilbert, who has a very pretty hand, will have to copy out the parts. Adrian, while I'm writing you must form the company.'

'You're right,' Adrian muttered. 'You have got the easy part.'

'Where do we find a company?' Hugh said. 'In here?' He gestured round the room; Gerald the innkeeper, Wat the plasterer, Jakey the gravedigger, Stephen and Martin from the shop and two dozen like them, few who had got beyond petty school and several who had not even that much learning. 'How many of them can read, let alone act?'

'Ask the most likely ones and see if they want to be players. If they can't read they can be taught their lines. Men who can't read have great memories.'

'How many do we need?' Adrian said. 'How many parts in this tragical history of yours?'

'As many parts as we have men to play them. If there are not enough they must double up. If there are too many they can be servants and rabble. I see Hugh here as Abe— as Arcturus, the good brother—'

'How do you fancy Wat for the bad one?'

'You know what he thinks of words on paper.'

Wat turned, brows lowered, and lumbered over. 'What whoreson took my name in vain?'

The three of them looked at him with edgy innocence.

'Why, Wat, we were wondering if you'd like to be in a play,' Adrian said.

'A play? Like *St George and the Dragon*?'

'Very like, but about real people.'

'What do you mean, real? When we go Mumming at Christmas I do St George as real as daylight.'

'Not saints and monsters,' Will said. 'People like us.'

'I've seen them at Corpus Christi, plays like that,' Wat said. 'I remember Lucifer falling arse over tit out of heaven.'

'Lucifer is not like us,' Hugh said, unwisely. 'He is king of the devils in hell.'

'Plenty of devils in here.' Wat leaned over them like a toppling chimney. 'You don't want common working men in your play, do you now? Men as can only read bricks and mortar.'

'Oh, we do,' Adrian said, hastily. 'Of course we do – anyone who wants to be of our company—'

'Ho, it's a company now, is it? Whose Men are you? Lord Worcester's? No place for the likes of us, then. I'll tell the lads to stay out of your way, Your Honours.' He clasped his cap beneath his chin and began to back away, bowing and scraping obsequiously.

'No, no.' Adrian grabbed at him. Wat could make a potent enemy. 'It's only ourselves, Stratford men.'

'Stratford boys.'

'All of us together; anyone's welcome who'd like to join us.'

'Well, I would,' the plasterer said. 'I'd like that right

well. Thank you for asking.' He beamed and went back to his friends.

'Now what have you done?' Hugh moaned feebly. 'We've got ourselves Wat for a player.'

'Where he leads others may follow. If he can't learn his part he can be a dumb servant or a turnip for all I care,' Will said. 'But that's the other thing you must do while I'm writing; find someone to be in charge.'

'A patron, you mean? As Wat said?'

'No, not a patron, but someone has to oversee it,' Will said, 'to be pageant master – book-holder I think it's called now, in the playhouses. He directs the players and finds the costumes and properties.'

'Costumes?' Hugh said. 'Are we to dress up as old Romans in sheets?'

'No, that would only confuse people.'

'So they needn't be old Romans at all?'

'They've got to be something,' Will said. 'If I make a play about Gaffer Hodge of Swine Street and his two sons who fall out, people will say, "Why go to a play? We can see all this at home." But if it is about old Romans and it happens in, oh, Syracuse, they'll go away thinking, "Those old Romans were just like us." '

'Whoever directs the players has to direct Wat,' Hugh said, looking over his shoulder at the workmen who were converging on the shovelboard again. 'Would you want to do that?'

'No, but I shan't have to. I'm writing it. Wat's not my headache. If you're agreed, though, to *The Tragedy of Cadmus and Arcturus*, I'll go home and start on it.'

Joan was rounding up her fowls for the night. She missed little Anne's happy chattering more than anyone, they had been so much together; now she talked to the hens. They were a poor replacement for her lost sister, but they clustered round her skirts, crooning and clucking while she crooned and clucked back at them. They all seemed to understand one another perfectly. Sir Solomon leered from the fence rail.

It was a mild evening. Gilbert lolled at the upstairs window of their bedchamber, officially learning his lesson and shying bits of broken plaster, that were migrating all over the house, at Will, where he sat on the bench beneath the elm, dipping his quill in and out of the ink but never quite managing to make a mark on his paper. As he had forecast, putting down what people said came easily. More difficult, much more difficult, was working out why they said it. Simple to write instructions for his characters' conduct; the problem was to explain why they behaved as they did.

Whoever had written the Glovers' Play had encountered the same problem. Holy Writ told him very little about what had happened between Cain and Abel, or why, so he had made Cain surly, foul-mouthed, foul-tempered, and when it came to making an offering to God he begrudged the best of his crop and sorted out the meanest sheaves for sacrifice. But why was he such a miserable son of a whore? The Bible gave no clues and the playwright had settled for making him like one of the Vices in the old Moral plays, bad because he was bad and he enjoyed being bad.

But that was not enough to explain Cain – no, Cadmus; he must stop thinking of him as Cain. But Cain was the prototype, son of Adam; God was practically his grandfather. *Why* did he hate Him and call Him evil names? Why did he hate his younger brother, hate him so much that he took up a weapon and slew him in the field?

A lump of plaster smacked into the tree trunk, inches from his ear. Will leaped up, grabbed a clod of earth and hurled it back, aiming for Gilbert's grin.

'Do that again and I'll break your neck!'

Gilbert saw what was coming and smartly closed the window so that the earth hit the glass instead, exploding into fragments. They both froze; a broken pane – Father would tear them limb from limb. Gilbert examined the glass, shook his head and sank out of sight, thumbing his nose. Will sat down again, groping for his thread of thought: Cain . . . Abel . . . younger brother . . .

Younger brother; suddenly he had it, the reason why. Cain, Cadmus, the elder brother, good and dutiful son who should have been the pride of his aged parents, the heir, inheritor of the land; and Abel, Arcturus, the younger – like Gilbert, the little bastard, not that he would ever murder Gilbert except by accident – for some reason the favourite. Father, in his old age, decides to make his will. Cadmus expects to receive the larger portion, as is his right, but the old man comes up with a mad unjust suggestion; the sons shall each have a farm. Whichever of them does best in the coming year shall have the greater inheritance.

As the year goes by Fate, or the stars – better leave God out of this altogether – Fate, then, all three Fates, conspire to make Cadmus fail. Wolves plunder his sheep, rats despoil his granaries. Cadmus sees that his father will reject him, goes by night to steal his brother's corn; Arcturus catches him, they come to blows.

Will was so eager to see how it would turn out he scarcely noticed that he had begun to write.

The Crofts' haberdashery shop was the one tidy room in the house where Adrian and his father had rattled around in easy-going disorder since Mistress Croft died. Adrian was sorting and pairing woollen stockings. Hugh, for whom women seemed to end at the neck and begin again at the instep, averted his eyes.

'So how many parts do we have to find players for now?' he said. 'This thing is growing all the time.'

30

Adrian told his fingers. 'Cadmus and wife; Arcturus and wife; Father – an ancient; Mother, who's been struck out twice and may not make it to the end; servant, Hodge, a knave; Hodge's dog—'

'We're to have a dog in this?'

'Well, we won't have any trouble finding one. Silvius, steward to Cadmus; the Fates—'

'How can we bring on the Fates?'

'Much as they do angels, I imagine.'

'I suppose it will be all three Fates. That's ten, possibly eleven, counting the dog. Are there to be sheep?'

'Why sheep?'

'Abel was a keeper of sheep.'

'Forget about Abel. This is not about Cain and Abel. God himself would not recognize this lot.'

'The name of the Lord—'

'I meant only, the Bible is the word of God. This play is the word of Will Shakespeare, it's a different thing altogether. Are you still sure you want to be in it?' Adrian said. Since his brothers had married and moved out he had been grateful for Hugh's company but he did not want him breathing his puritan objections to the play down their necks. It would be like having Cato the Censor along for the ride.

'Well, so far it is only I, and Wat the plasterer. Is he still to play Cadmus?'

'I don't know. Cadmus has a lot to say by the looks of it. Wat could handle the brawling and smiting, but this Cadmus is turning out to be a subtle man who thinks deeply. And then there's his wife—'

'And that's another thing,' Hugh said, 'all these wives.'

'Only two, and perhaps the mother.'

'We have to find boys to play them whose voices have not broken.'

'That lets you and me out.'

'They may not want to play women. How if they are mocked by their friends, afterwards?'

'Why should they be?' Adrian said. 'People know the difference between play-acting and real life, or the man who was Lucifer would be whipped out of town and the man who played God would be worshipped even while he was out in the fields spreading muck.'

'That was in the Corpus Christi plays. This is not being done for the glory of God.'

'Essex's Men play women.'

'That's their craft. They are paid.'

'Well, Gilbert Shakespeare has a lad's voice still. Will can persuade him if all else fails; take him warmly by the throat, as one does a brother . . .'

The door of the shop opened and Master Croft looked in.

'Father?'

'There's a council meeting tomorrow. What do I tell them?'

'That all is in hand. Will's writing the play—'

'Will? Writing it? I thought it was already written. What about the playbook?'

'It was an old thing,' Adrian said. 'The mice had been at it. All that was left would scarcely have lasted a quarter-hour.'

'Wasn't it *The Slaying of Abel*? Is Will patching it?'

'It was past patching. He's writing a new play about two Roman brothers.'

'Can he do it? Surely he's never written a play before?'

'He seems to be enjoying it,' Adrian said.

'I dare say he is, but will anyone else enjoy it? Are people going to pay to see something that young Will ran up before supper one evening?'

'I don't think it will be like that,' Adrian said. 'We've all seen plays. Will's been to Coventry; we read the old Romans at school.'

'So did I. Will's no Plautus. Still, if you're sure . . .?'

'I'm sure.' Adrian was edging him out of the room. 'The council will have to approve it, won't they?'

'Some of us must read it, yes, but if Will does a good job I don't think you need worry too much. Tell him to hold back on the sedition and blasphemy.'

'If the council do approve, will they vote us money to do it?'

'What will you need?'

'We don't know yet. But there will have to be costumes and properties.'

'You can borrow a lot of those, surely. Will you have music?'

'Must have, people will be disappointed if we don't.' As far as he knew, Will had not planned any singing parts, but servants and rabble could burst into song at appropriate moments. 'If we can find a pipe-and-tabor man there could be dancing. Otherwise it will be Jakey and his damned bagpipe. Another thing, Dad; where should we put it on?'

'Where do you want to put it on?'

'We haven't got that far. But we couldn't do it on a pageant cart even if we had a pageant cart.'

'You want an inn yard? It had better be worth it.'

'It will be easier for the players,' Adrian said. 'They won't be like the old guildsmen who were used to working on carts. They could tip Lucifer out of heaven, part the Red Sea, drown the whole world and float an Ark on the waters, all on a cart. I think our people will need more room.'

'And just who are your people?' Robert Croft asked, curiously.

'Hugh and I are working on that,' Adrian said, and

added, with more optimism than he felt, 'after all, we've got the whole town to choose from.'

'Get moving, then. You haven't long to do the choosing and then your players have to learn their parts and how to say them.'

'You wouldn't like to be in it, would you? There's a part for an aged father.'

'A drivelling dotard, I suppose.'

'Well, yes, he has grown old and foolish.'

His father smacked him affectionately round the head. 'You'd better find someone so old and foolish that he doesn't know what he's letting himself in for.'

Three

A hood looked over the churchyard wall. Out of the tail of his eye Adrian saw a sinewy hand wrapped around a staff, a glint of white cheekbone underlining a hollow eye socket in the cavern of the hood, and recognized Death come to claim them, all and some.

'Then the Fates speak,' Will said, oblivious. 'Cadmus takes them for three old women going to market.'

The other hand, a branch of ill-knit bones, extended over the wall and pointed. Adrian felt the marrow of his own bones congeal, the sun-warmed stones at his back grew chill. It was a bright balmy evening, they sat among may buds and fragrant vernal grass, the best of the spring was before them, but the charnel house was not ten yards away and they all knew what lay beneath the turf where they were sitting. *In the midst of life we are in death.* On a single day a man might rise at dawn in good health, dance at his wedding, bed his bride, get a child and die before midnight.

Hugh had also seen. Through white lips he gasped, 'Will, for God's sake—'

The hood spoke. 'In the name of Christ, masters, direct me to the holy brothers.'

Will finally turned and saw what was behind him. The voice from the hood went on: 'I came by Studley and all was ruin. I came by Kenilworth and the roof was gone. In Warwick grass grows where they used to stand and sing.'

Adrian relaxed a little. The thin voice was plaintive, old – and human. 'Show yourself.'

The hood was pushed back to reveal a head with living hair, not a skull with wisps adhering to shreds of scalp. There were eyes in the sunken sockets. Will stood up.

'Is that David the harper from Caernarfon?'

'I was David the harper.'

Was? Adrian felt the chill descend again. He remembered the Welshman from childhood, big, vigorous, with a voice that could fill a hall. *Was?*

'Don't you play any more?'

'I was bewitched.'

On cue, another head rose horribly from behind the wall. This one wore a younger face under a bee-skep of hair lopped off as if with shears at jaw level.

'How many more of you?' Will said. Hugh was shuffling nervously, Adrian still twitching from his

37

first grim imaginings. Will sounded unfazed.

'Only we two. This is Adam of Muscovy,' the harper who was no longer a harper said.

Only two; two lunatics; Tom o' Bedlam and his father.

'Let them go,' Adrian muttered. 'Let them find their brothers in this world or the next.'

'The poor old fool's looking for a monastery,' Will said. 'He wants a place to sleep.'

'He looks more as if he wants a place to die in.'

'Davy, the monks are long gone,' Will said, 'forty years or more.'

The harper blinked uncertainly. 'I remember now. The King drove them out.'

'I told him so,' Adam of Muscovy said. He did not sound as though he had ever been closer to Muscovy than Warwick. 'But it's what keeps him going. Every evening as it grows dark, he thinks he will come to a religious house where the brothers will take us in.'

'There's no religious house here, never was,' Hugh said.

'Why, I know that, but then, I know where I am,' Adam said. 'Is this not Stratford, on Avon River?'

David climbed down his staff, hand over hand, and sat on the grass on the other side of the wall. The staff remained upright, the only evidence of his presence. Adam leaned on the coping stones.

'Can he really not play any longer?' Adrian said.

'Never a note, but it wasn't witchcraft. Look at the swelling in his finger joints. That comes with old age, with being always out of doors in foul weather, but he had words with a woman over a missing hen and lost the skill of his hands soon after. He thinks she ill-wished him. He seems to know you, or rather, you seem to know him.'

'He used to play at our Christmas revels,' Will said. 'We looked forward to his coming, he was well-liked. But how do you know him, who are you?'

'I was the fool in a great house,' Adam said, with a certain pride, as if he had claimed to have been master of a great house. 'I did very well when I was antic and fantastical, but I'm antic only by turns. For whole months at a time I was the greatest fool that ever lived; tumbling, singing, tricks to cozen the eye, never still, I could keep going all night. I still can,' he added, 'but in between the fooling fits I'm as grave as a Parson. I don't know how it is, there's nothing I can do about it. My lord was very patient, he understood; when the antic fit was on me, he said, it paid for the times between, and let me go where I would, always welcomed me back, but he took a new young wife and my lady soon tired of me. "Adam," she'd say, "come, let's have some fooling at dinner," and when the fit was on me, and it was on me for months, as I said, I could fool all through dinner and on all night until breakfast, and I did, even if there was none left awake to watch me, but when the fit left me I could not stir to raise a smile, not even on my own face, nor lift a foot to cut a step, and she would rant and rail for never so long, it made no difference. In the end she said to my lord, "What's the profit in keeping a fool who's only a fool by the seasons? Whether he's fooling or not, he keeps eating," although I swear by the Holy Rood I ate scarce enough to keep the heart in my bosom beating, and at last she persuaded him, ranting and railing, to turn me out of doors. When the antic fit came on me again, back I went, as I had always done, but she had the doors barred against me and the dogs let loose. So now I walk the roads whether the antic fit is on me or not.'

They were all gasping when he had finished, from holding their breaths, as if a violent spring hail had beaten them speechless. At last Will said, 'Is the antic fit on you now or are you in sober season?'

'What do you think?' Adam said. 'When I'm sad I can scarce string together enough words to make a Collar of Esses: string . . . sing . . . sob . . . sigh, spit, snap snarl shriek squeal screech scream swinge swive—'

'Are you really from Muscovy?' Adrian chipped in, before he could get going again.

'No, Evesham. But for a time I fell in with a travelling company, Lord Edgware's Men—'

'Did they ever play here?' Hugh asked.

'Not likely. You're accustomed to the real thing in Stratford, no doubt, real companies from London. We, I say we because while I was with them I was one of them, we went to little towns where they knew no more of London but that it wasn't over the next hill. You could call yourself the Queen's Men or Lord Derby's Men, and they wouldn't argue if they wanted to see a play. But our leader had settled on Lord Edgware because he'd been there and it wasn't big enough to have an earl and no one north of Watford would have heard of it.'

'Where's Watford?' Hugh said.

'Why Muscovy?' Adrian asked. 'Did you just like the sound of it?'

'Don't you like the sound of it? Muscovy, Tartary, Hungary, Sicily . . . all names that don't sound like anywhere else. We fell in once with a shipman and he'd met men from Muscovy. We asked him was it true that their heads grow beneath their shoulders or have they one great foot that they hold over their heads to fend off the heat of the sun, and he said no, they looked as other men, but he said they had hair like mine, straight as straw, thick as thatch and the same colour. "You could be a Muscovite," he said to me, and it took the fancy of the others, so after that when we came to a town they'd announce me as a special attraction, Adam of Muscovy, and I'd dance a jig like any Englishman born, but believing I was from beyond the sea people thought I did a strange foreign dance. "Very gloomy and violent those Muscovites are," the shipman said. I can do gloomy and violent when the fit's on me.'

'And just gloomy when it isn't?' Will said. '*Are* you violent?'

'Only in show.'

'So you've been a player.'

'Oh, yes,' Adam said. 'I played many parts, but showed up best in the gloomy and violent ones.'

'You can learn to say a part?'

'Oh my God,' Adrian whispered.

'When the fit's on me.'

'And how long have you been in this present fantastical fit?' Will asked.

'Not above a seven-night. It's a great relief to me when I feel it coming on, and it does truly seem to run with the seasons, for about the time we hear the first cuckoo I feel the vapours of my heavy fit rise up and leave me like a cloud. It is the heaviness that holds me down,' Adam said, 'as if I shall sink into the earth like draining water. I shall be in this antic fit now until after harvest, God willing. The doctors say that every man has his humour, but it seems to me that I have two, sanguineous in spring, as nature intended, and creeping melancholy as the year wanes. It is a grievous complexion, masters. Grievous.'

Adrian peered over the wall to where David the

Welsh harper was still sitting, the staff raised beside him like a standard. Was Will planning to make a part for a holy madman too? The country roads were thronged with the mad, the poor, the poor pretending to be mad, and this vagabond claiming to be a player from a company travelling under false colours; all of them destitute and relying for charity upon the goodwill of their fellow men since King Henry had destroyed the monasteries, where almoner monks had cared for the dispossessed.

Adam of Muscovy did not look so very mad, but traces of his melancholy humour still hung about him.

'How did you meet, you never told us.'

'We were whipped out of Daventry as sturdy beggars on the same day,' Adam said, 'when he had lost his skill and I was in my heavy fit so deep I could not conjure up a lie to save my skin. Sturdy! Look at him. But you might say we are both wandering in our wits, so we wander together.'

'And you think you'll be merry till Pentecost?'

'It's only just past Easter. I told you, the antic fit comes with the cuckoo and flies with the swallows.'

Will was foraging in his purse. He brought out coins. 'Go to the Bear in Bridge Street and say to Gerald the host that Adrian Croft and Will Shakespeare sent you and that you are working with us for our Whitsun pastime. If any man raises a hand against you, tell him that.'

'Are you making game of us?' Adam said, taking the coins first. 'What will you do for your pastime at Whitsun, put us in a ring and bait us like bears? Are we to be sport for the town?'

'No. We three here are putting on a play and we have need of advice from one who knows the business of it. Thursday is Market Day. You'll find me at the glover's stall by the High Cross.'

Adam stooped down to rouse David the harper and soon after the hooded head and the tawny thatch were seen moving away down the lane towards the town.

'I don't believe you did that,' Hugh said. Will was leaning on the wall, watching his protégés leave. 'You've just hired two vagrant madmen to wreck our play.'

'I couldn't let him go,' Will said. 'Didn't you hear him, the things he said? About the chain made up of links like Ss, such as a knight wears. I want to study his speech. And where else am I going to meet a man who falls in and out of two humours?'

'Why would you want to?' Adam said.

'Gloomy and violent,' Will said, rapturously. 'That's what I need. He's the very pattern for Cadmus.'

Oh, to be a schoolman in Oxford, with quiet cloisters and a cell where he could shut the door on all distractions and be alone with his thoughts.

There was no place in the house where he could

work undisturbed, except the glove shop, and Father would never allow him in there with his ink. He could hear the old man down there now, shouting at Martin who was never afraid to shout back. Wat was doing running repairs around the chimney in the big front room, Gilbert and Dick were rough-housing in the bedchamber, and Mother had driven him out of the kitchen as soon as she saw the ink. At this rate he would end up in the henhouse with Joan. Joan thought that it was wonderful that he should be writing a play. She was the only one who did, but she would keep asking questions. 'Will there be lovers in it? Will there be a marriage? Oh, do have a marriage, and dancing.'

In desperation he settled at the top of the stairs, candlewax in his ears to block Dick's shrieking. He struck heavy lines through the words he had written for Cadmus and the Fates. Even one Fate was proving a nuisance. In the Mystery plays you could bring on God and his angels; the Moral plays had Vices and demons, but the way *Cadmus and Arcturus* was shaping up, there was little place for anything that was not of the earth, earthy. He was not even sure if he could get away with bringing on a ghost.

Cadmus must not be the plaything of Fate or blind Fortune; it was not enough to make him ill-natured and envious because the machinations of the play required it. This was a man given to brooding and muttering, fancying conspiracies against himself, convinced that his brother was fawning deceitfully on their father and perhaps casting sheep's eyes at Cadmus's wife who would, of course, be innocent. He tried to make Cadmus brawl and rail, as planned, but all that came to mind was the spectacle of King Herod, raging up and down the streets of Coventry during *The Slaughter of the Innocents*, yelling 'I rant! I rave! And now I run mad!' which had scared the daylights out of him when he was a child, but now returned as a figure of base comedy. Cadmus must terrify in his fury; one touch of the Herods and people might laugh.

Herod had come in roaring and blaspheming. If Cadmus did the same, much as Cain had done, he would be expected to carry on in the same vein throughout the play. He would become tedious, there would be no reason to wait and see what happened to him; someone like that was obviously destined for a bad end. The only way to surprise the audience would be to have him right in his suspicions all along. If he began amiable and pleasant and descended into rage and murderous madness, that *would* surprise them.

Will sat gnawing his pen, a bad habit that had spoiled many quills. Why did he want to surprise the audience? They would not be expecting a surprise, was it safe to spring one on them? They might decide to feel they had been cheated and throw things . . . but if he were to confound their expectations slowly, before their eyes, so that they could see and hear it happening, they might just wonder admiringly at the sight of a man who could swing from one humour to another. Those Muscovites Adam had spoken of seemed to inhabit two humours at once, gloomy and violent. How many people did he know personally who were in the same humour all the time? His father was more crabbed than he used to be since the business began to go downhill, but not all the time. His rages were no more than outbursts, unpredictable but brief.

Perhaps we all swing a little, he thought, like the needle on a shipman's card, shivering and hesitating, northwest, nor'nor'east, but always in the end pointing to our own true north, whatever that might be. So if a man's compass failed him, and north became south and his needle could find no rest, we would watch him groping, bewildered, unable to see his way, casting about in his private darkness, eyes fixed on a wandering planet that he took for the Pole star.

Could he make Cadmus in such a fashion, so that even Wat the plasterer would be transfixed with wondering what might become of this unhappy man, at odds with Fortune?

Then he remembered that Wat would not be in the audience. Wat was going to be in the play.

★   ★   ★

'There's papers in here somewhere, I threw them in myself,' Adrian said, delving up to the elbows in the oak chest at the foot of the stairs. When shelves overflowed the surplus found its way there, whatever it might be.

'What are you looking for?' Hugh sat on the window seat, out of the way of the churning.

'Will's running out of paper. We'll have no play if there's nothing to write it on.'

'If he had less paper he might make an end of it sooner,' Hugh said. He consulted his list. 'How many parts now? Cadmus and Arcturus, Mistress Cadmus, Mistress Arcturus, their father, their mother, a servant, a dog, the Fates—'

'No, the Fates have gone – and so's the dog, thank God. Strike out the dog. We are to have no Fates, not even one Fate. Since we met the man from Muscovy Will has come up with another idea.'

'He's from Evesham,' Hugh said. 'Whatever they may be like in Muscovy they are Englishmen in Evesham. My aunt Hopkin lives in Evesham.'

'Well, wherever . . . Cadmus is not to be mad seven days in the week. He is driven mad, or drives himself mad. You needn't worry, Will thinks that you should play Arcturus and he is the same all through, a good man, pious in his habits.'

'I wish he'd make his mind up. So far we have you and me – are you to be in it?'

'I suppose so.'

'Quite, you don't know. You, me, Adam of Muscovy if the wind doesn't change and blow his wits inside out, Wat the plasterer, Gilbert Shakespeare if Will can persuade or frighten him into it – what about Will? Is he going to be a player?'

'He may have to be at this rate. We still must find two more women and someone to play the father, the Duke of Hungary.'

'Hungary! I thought they were old Romans.'

'Not any more. You must be patient—'

'What's the point of being patient? We can be patient till Ascension Day with a week left to learn our parts and rehearse them.'

'Will's play is coming new all the time. It's not the Glovers' Play any more, *The Slaying of Abel.*'

'Why Hungary? Where is Hungary, anyway?'

'I don't know. Somewhere beyond France – here, isn't this the shoe you lost last Christmas?'

'I hope not, it's growing green fur. Stop grubbing about. Are they Romans in Hungary?'

'Holy Romans, perhaps. But it doesn't matter. What matters is that they are not local men. No one can point the finger and say, "That old man is Sir Edward Greville and those are his sons." '

'What are we supposed to do while Will decides about his Holy Hungarians?'

49

'Suit yourself,' Adrian said, closing the chest. 'I'm going to the Bear to play shove-groat.'

'Isn't the mad Muscovite staying at the Bear, of Will's charity?'

'Yes. To tell the truth, Will asked me to look in and make sure that he's still there.'

'You're not supposed to come into the shop. Why aren't you helping Mother in the dairy?' Will said, without raising his head from his stitching. He knew his sister was behind him by the gulping and sniffing. He had been dreading this moment. He felt the force of her anguish before she could open her mouth.

'*Is that Dorcas?*'

On the bench at his elbow Will and his father had raised a ghastly gibbet, a frame of hatter's wire, something like a chimney with a farthingale beneath it. Over it was stretched a pale pimply skin, lardy yellow-white and blue-flushed. Joan gazed at it, eyes welling.

'She was taken sick in the night,' Will said.

'How do you know? You never go near the hens, that's my work.'

'I could see her from here . . .' he pointed out of the window '. . . with her poor legs stiff and stark in the air as if she clutched at the stars with her claws.'

His poetical fancy was wasted on Joan. She was all feeling.

'No you couldn't!'

No, he couldn't. Unfortunately, since he had last looked towards the hen run the spring foliage had obscured the view.

'Well, not from here exactly. It was Father who found her. She was old, Joanie. How long is it since she laid an egg?'

'Thursday.'

Damn! They must have got the wrong one. 'Oh . . . well, she hadn't laid many lately, had she? She was well stricken in years.'

'And why have you put her on that horrible – *thing*? What is it?'

'Hen's leather is very difficult to tan—'

'You're going to make her into gloves!'

'No, Dorcas shall not be made into gloves. But, Joan, you must understand, we've had an order, from an important person, a rich man, he wants to give his sweetheart chicken-skin gloves rolled up in a walnut. Oh Christ!'

'What?'

'I have to find the walnut. Anyway, none of us knows how to tan chicken skin so we have to try our skill with a hide before we get fine hens and cut out the gloves.' Poor Joan, too young to be consulted, too old for kindly lies.

'Dorcas was a fine hen.'

'She was, she laid fine eggs, but God put hens on earth for the good of mankind, didn't he? The same as the goats and sheep. You don't weep for the poor kid when you see us cut out cheveril, or pray for the poor sheep when we make them into belts and purses. How should we have sausages without the poor pigs?'

'But she knew me. She used to come when I called.'

'They all come when you call. They know you have grain for them.'

'Not Dorcas. She used to sit in my lap – oh!'

As if things were not bad enough, Dick had to wander past the window clasping the yellow scaly feet of the late Dorcas. Will had given them to him to play with as he seemed to have his eye on them. Now he could see why. By pulling the tendons in the legs, Dick could make the claws open and shut in grotesquely life-like fashion. As they watched, he stooped and made them pick up pebbles. Joan gave a last howl and rushed out. Will looked sourly at Dorcas's skin stretched on its gibbet. Because they were trying to keep the stitching to a minimum they could not pin it out flat to cure. The frame, by preserving the shape of the neck, had turned a comely fowl into a nasty bulbous creature with no head but two empty flaccid thighs and the pathetic stump of gristle that had once been her tail.

Poor Dorcas, this was an ungrateful end for a good and faithful servant. It was a mistake to give names to animals as if they were fellow Christians, but how could you help it? Whoever owned a dog without giving it a name to call it by?'

Four

Adrian waylaid the schoolboys as they left the Guildhall and scattered both ways along Church Street. The little ones came out first as if shot from a cannon, moving too fast to intercept, but he was not interested in recruiting children – yet. For all he knew, by the time he returned to Henley Street Will could have bestowed a family on Cadmus and his wife, perhaps Arcturus too. At least he was keeping women to a minimum. However elaborate his fancies became, he had the sense to remember that good women were hard to find.

Adrian was loitering outside the Grammar School in search of good women, or rather a couple of lads with unbroken voices who might be good at playing women. Gilbert had assented, under pressure, on condition that he got to play the woman with the least to say, on the grounds that a faint shadow was appearing on his upper lip and his voice might go at any moment. Adrian listened keenly to the conversations of the older boys, instantly dismissing those whose voices threatened to crack or who were growling already. He was still desperately short of players to accommodate Will's ever-multiplying Hungarians. He might need even the growlers.

Giles Butcher: a sweet melifluous treble, but at fourteen he already looked thirty and was a yard across the shoulders. His nose was broken too, generously plastered across his beaming face. No one, not even a man of two humours, would have taken him to wife.

Anthony Stone: fair and slender, a voice that although unbroken was naturally deep. Probably it never would break but sink gracefully into a permanent curtsey; worth risking. Henry Fielden: nigh on six feet but pretty enough except for a vicious squint that made him approach everything sideways like a coney-catcher. Philip Thacker – no, already shaving and with such an Adam's apple that he seemed to have swallowed an egg that had lodged in his throat.

These four were sauntering towards Corn Street. He had to make a start somewhere and casually crossed the way to fall into step with them. Four years ago he had been one of them, and they little boys on the lowest forms. They knew him, with luck they might still feel a touch of deference.

'What do you want?' Giles Butcher turned, with his air of bovine truculence. He could not say 'Good morrow' without seeming to be looking for a fight and yet his voice betrayed him.

'How should you like to be in a play?' Adrian said, coming straight to the point. Schoolboys, after all, did not appreciate or respond to the normal courtesies.

'What, me?' Giles said.

'All of you.' They didn't *have* to be women . . .

'We are acting Seneca at this moment – in school,' Philip said. The egg bobbed and convulsed alarmingly as his voice vaulted from boom to bat-squeak.

'This is not old Romans. The council wants a pastime at Whitsun and some of us are putting on a play.'

'Mumming?'

'Not mumming, neither. This is a real play, such as Essex's Men give us, only we are doing it for ourselves.'

'We?'

'William Shakespeare's writing it.'

'Is that supposed to mean it will be any good?' Anthony said. Oh, he had a lovely voice, even when he was being rude. 'What does Will know about writing plays?'

'I've seen it – some of it. He's still writing. It is good. The council have voted nine shillings and seven pence to pay—'

'We'll be paid?'

'No, not the players. But these things cost money to put on. We shall do it for sport.'

'Where's the sport in learning words? We do enough of that already.' Henry looked him squarely in the ear.

Adrian tried to ignore the squint. The voice was mercifully far from breaking.

'It's not just learning words, there are actions too. It is about two brothers who fall out.' He hoped it was still about two brothers who fell out. 'There is a murder.'

That got their interest.

'Who dies?'

'The good brother.'

'Is there a battle, are there soldiers in it?'

'Very likely.' Very likely indeed, did they but know it. Will could sow his dragon seed and whole armies might spring up overnight, like mushrooms.

'I wouldn't want to be the good brother,' Giles said.

Adrian forbore to enlighten them about the exact parts he had in mind. 'My cousin Hugh Burnet is to play the good brother.'

'And he dies? That's all right, then,' Giles said. 'Good persons are passing dull.'

Will had reached very much the same conclusion himself. As far as he was concerned, the death of Arcturus could not come too soon. As a character he was a cipher, he had nothing to do but *be* good, dutiful son, comradely brother, thrifty hardworking farmer, loving husband. Cadmus was far more interesting to construct, he was almost creating himself, skulking about, complaining of his father, spying on his brother, threatening his wife because he fancied that Arcturus was paying her unseemly attentions.

But what if Arcturus really were neglecting his own wife and child – they could use Dick for the child if he could be persuaded to leave off playing with his hen's feet for five minutes. He went about picking things up with them. Joan had not spoken to Will for three days.

Yes; if Arcturus were not the saintly figure he seemed he might really be deceiving their father and casting covetous glances at Cadmus's wife. So Cadmus would have good reason for his suspicions; but then he would not be a villain.

There was no real need for him to be a villain. In fact, to make him a villain was almost too easy. Villains, Will was beginning to discover, were a deal more fun to create. They made things happen. If Cadmus were an upright man, driven to madness, his downfall would be all the greater, and when Arcturus's smug phantom rose from the grave to pursue him, the sympathy of the audience would be as much with Cadmus as with the slaughtered innocent – who would be much less innocent than those about him had imagined. Only the audience would know the truth; that would please them.

Well yes, of course, were Arcturus wholly good, as soon as his brother slew him his soul would rise straight to heaven in the arms of angels – Will really could not be bothered to bring on an angel. But if Arcturus had sins upon his conscience and died unshriven, then his ghost would be condemned to suffer in purgatory and walk the earth at appointed hours. Hugh was sure to raise objections at the mention of unshriven souls and purgatory but they all, Hugh included, knew that the dead walked. And all this was happening safely in foreign parts, Popish foreign parts or even heathen. If Hugh refused to play the ghost he would do it himself in a sheet, face covered. Hugh topped him by several inches, and stooped, a camelopard to Will's ox, but in the excitement of seeing a ghost walk the audience would never notice.

His quill was sucked down to the nib and he had bitten the draggled shaft into a series of Zs. He took out his pen knife to cut another, forcing himself to pare carefully at the feather, carving a fine point. Goose quills were easy enough to come by but he was using up paper at an alarming rate, all those experiments and false starts and dead ends, on the backs of old bills and receipts, patterns, letters. Soon he would have to settle to the story he wanted to tell about the people he had created – Yes, Hugh, just like God – and make a straight run at it, start to finish, without changing his mind every few lines. He had not let Adrian know how far he was from actually starting, let alone finishing. If only he could get the names right. He had tossed out Cadmus and Arcturus on the spur of the moment, as substitutes for Cain and

Abel, but these quarrelsome brothers were not called Cadmus and Arcturus. He sensed them waiting sullenly in the next room. 'When you can take the trouble to learn our names,' they seemed to be saying, 'then we'll come out and do your bidding.'

And when his work was done the parts must be written out with cues and directions. Gilbert wrote best, and fastest, but he had not yet been informed that he was going to do it. He had been coaxed, cajoled, nagged, bullied into taking part at all, especially when he divined why they wanted him. Gilbert was unnaturally sharp. 'It's only for my voice,' he said. 'You have the voice of an angel,' Will assured him, 'and if you do not agree to play for us I'll stake you out like Saint Erasmus and unreel your guts with a windlass.'

No, no more bullying of Gilbert. He must be made to feel a valued member of the company and, truly, they were beginning to be a company; himself, Adrian, Hugh, Gilbert and three or four of his schoolfellows who did not yet know what was likely to befall them, and Wat, and Adam of Muscovy who must play the aged father, so long as his predictions about the length of his antic fit were accurate. He seemed to have settled in at the Bear, his conversation sought after for his stock of stories and his prodigious ability to keep talking. The torrent of words that had near overwhelmed them on that first evening, when he arose beside the churchyard wall with

Davy the harper, showed no signs of drying up, although it was slowing down. He could talk the clock round. Will was relying on the truth of his claim to have been a company player, if only one of the deeply suspect Earl of Edgware's Men. It was on the strength of this presumed expertise that part of the council's nine and sevenpence was maintaining him at the Bear. If he had been a player he would be able to learn his part. If he had not, it was quite likely that he would be able to say only the kinds of things that he said already. In which case his part, when it was written out, would have to be written in the style of Adam of Muscovy to be spoken apparently without pause for breath.

Robert Croft's haberdashery stall was across the way from the Shakespeares' glove stall in the market place, at the foot of the cross. Both commodities were in demand and morning trade was brisk. Adrian looked across from time to time, and saw Will surrounded, mostly by women and young girls, the latter not necessarily there to buy. They liked Will because he let them try things on even when he knew that they could not possibly afford them. He seemed to stand in a little garden of uplifted hands, turning and preening like flowers in a light breeze, as gloves were held up for his opinion. Adrian knew what he was saying: 'A perfect fit. Only a hand like yours could make a work of leather into a work of art. No, not that pair, sweetheart. Your tapering fingers would become bears' paws. Try these.'

He had a pretty turn of phrase, but a hand and a glove were, perforce, much the same shape whereas a well-laced corset could turn a butter churn into an hourglass.

The girls cooed and flirted under his flattery, never noticing that he rarely looked at them, only at the gloves, and his mind was on neither. His conversation was basically sales patter by rote, even when there was no prospect of a sale. Away from the stall he wasted none of his sweet talk on girls; if he were not working in the shop he was reading. There could scarcely be a book in Stratford that he had not borrowed at some time, and none of the girls they knew wanted to spend precious leisure talking about books. Adrian's own Katherine Page, as near to a sweetheart as he had ever had, had grown noticeably cooler since he and Will had embarked upon the play.

'Tell me about it when it's done,' she said, 'and I'll come and see it.'

He had tried to convey to her the astonishing thing that was happening in their presence, how Will had taken the nibbled relics of the northcountryman's play, *The Slaying of Abel*, and made it into a stirring drama of jealousy, rivalry, mistrust and murder.

Adrian prayed that it would be a stirring drama. It was currently entitled *Two Noble Brothers* and Will had read bits to him to find out how they sounded. Of what he could remember he relayed fragments to Katherine. She was not impressed.

'Wouldn't you want to be part of it if you could?' he wheedled.

'In a play!' He might have said a whorehouse.

'You have a sweet voice, Kate. You could sing.' He was becoming a discerning judge of voices.

'Go to your play.' She boxed his ears. 'Come back to me when it's over, if I haven't tired of waiting. Stephen Thacker has time to spare for a girl.'

Stephen, Philip's elder brother, worked in John Shakespeare's shop. Will had commended his light tenor voice, which might be persuaded higher, and lack of inches, as promising female material. Be that as it might, he was man enough to have his eye on Adrian's girl.

'I think he's going to be in the play too.'

Katherine hit him again and he had not seen her since except in church, ostentatiously looking in every direction but his, except when she squinnied round to see if he were looking at her.

Will had no girl to offend with his self-absorption. He seemed more at ease with women; he was, at least, able to look them in the eye. One was talking to him now, old enough to be his mother – no, that was not quite fair, but she was no girl. On the other hand she was certainly going to buy. Will had left off sweet-talking and was evidently clinching the deal. The crowd around both stalls was thinning, people were drifting towards dinner. Adrian left the other apprentice in charge of the stall and walked over to the cross. The woman was just leaving, wearing her purchase. Not a working girl, then. She carried her hands unnaturally high, admiring them.

'How near done are you?'

'Done what? No, those will never fit. These are more slender.' Will deftly abstracted a pair of kidskins from a girl with hands like muck rakes and tactfully replaced them with a pair she could not split.

'The play,' Adrian said. 'We don't have so very much time left. When can I call the company together so that you can read it to them and we can allot the parts?'

'Saturday?'

'You'll have finished it by then?'

'Near enough.'

'Monday, then. To make sure it *is* finished.'

'The body of it is done. We may need a prologue and an epilogue, but I can do those as we go along. If it weren't a tragedy it could end with a dance.'

'Maybe a tragedy is too heavy for a Whitsun pastime,' Adrian said. 'Can you fashion a happy ending?'

'With one brother dead and the other fled into exile pursued by a ghost?'

'Do we have to have a ghost?'

'Do you want me to go back and start it all again?'
Will demanded. He was not going to relinquish his best
effect. 'No ghost, no murder, no falling out between
brothers, no dotard father?'

'How doting is the father?'

'Not so much as he was. Things have changed a bit
since you last saw it.'

'You don't say.'

'The father wants his sons to help rule his dukedom
and promises that the one who does best will be his
heir.'

'By law the elder must be, surely?'

'They're twins,' Will said swiftly.

'Is their mother living still?'

'Still?'

'Well, you do kill people off when you find you don't
need them,' Adrian said. 'The mother's fallen to your
pen twice already.'

'She has risen from the dead.' Will grinned. 'The
Duchess is yet living.'

'Is she still of child-bearing age?'

'She could be.'

'Then let one come in at the end and say, "The
Duchess, my lord, is delivered of a son," and you can
bring on the babe, or something like it, wrapped up.
After all, in the original—'

'What original?'

'The Book of Genesis. After Abel was slain, Eve bore another son—'

'Seth! Of course. This babe will be a consolation in their old age and a cause for rejoicing even though one son is dead and the other's in exile. Oh, well done, Adrian.'

'Exactly. So you can end with a merry dance, can't you?'

'I shall have to write in something earlier about the Duchess expecting a child. We can't have a servant come in and say, "The Duchess, my lord, hath borne a babe," if no one knew it was likely to happen.'

'Just put in a line or two,' Adrian begged. 'Don't rewrite the whole thing again. Will Monday give you long enough? Hullo, you've got another customer.'

A gentleman had come up to the stall while they were talking.

'What's this about a play? Are Lord Worcester's Men coming to town?'

Adrian and Will knew money when they saw it.

'Not so far as we know. This is our own play, to be put on as a Whitsun pastime.'

'Your own play? You're presenting it yourselves?' The gentleman seemed to find this amusing.

'I'm writing it,' Will said. 'Adrian here is the book-holder.'

'Am I? Oh, yes; I am. We've formed a company.'

'Really? At Whitsun? I must make sure to attend and bring some friends. What is it called, this play of yours?'

'*The Tragical History of Honorius and Francisco*,' Will said.

Honorius and Francisco? Adrian thought. Who the hell were they? What had become of Cadmus and Arcturus?

'That sounds like a heavy business for a pastime.'

'It's not all tragedy,' Will said.

'I'm glad to hear it. Do you by any chance have time to make gloves when you're not play-writing?'

Will fanned his hand across the stall. 'Whatever you will – and we take orders.'

'You have taken an order. Do the words chicken and skin jog your memory?'

'You're Master Starling?' Will said. 'Chicken-skin gloves in a walnut, wasn't it? A pretty notion.'

'Has it got any further than being a notion?'

'As a matter of fact, my father is cutting a trial glove at this moment. We don't normally work with hens, you understand. We have cured a skin – if you go to our house in Henley Street he'll be pleased to show you.'

'Are you sure he'll be pleased?'

'Once we've determined the kind of thread we'll procure a couple of fine capons and set to work.'

'Good.' Master Starling moved off. 'I'm glad to know that my gloves have not got in the way of your writing.'

They watched him tread elegantly through the market.

'Bastard.'

'My sister's favourite hen died for his sake. If I'd known what he was like I'd have practised on a crow. So, he'll bestow his poxy presence on our play, will he?'

'I didn't like the sound of that,' Adrian said. 'I don't think he means to come to enjoy it.'

'I know what he meant. What's a glover's apprentice doing writing plays?'

'Or a haberdasher's apprentice directing them. There's no lout like a well-bred lout.'

'We're as well-learned as he is. We'd both be at Oxford now if our fathers could have afforded it. Let's hope he's lettered enough to know good writing when he hears it.'

'You think it's good?'

'I'd have left off long ago if I didn't,' Will said. 'It could be better, no doubt, but it's not bad.'

'Who are Honorius and Francisco? What was wrong with Cadmus and Arcturus?'

'Oh, I never meant to stick with those names,' Will said. 'We were thinking of old Romans then, to silence Hugh. I couldn't bring Cadmus and Arcturus to life. It's strange; these are not real persons but the names had to be right. Once I hit on Honorius and Francisco I was well away.'

'Not so strange,' Adrian said. 'What's more important to a man than his name? I don't care for mine overmuch, but if another man speaks it wrongly I'm mortally offended. If he can not get my name right it is as if he does not care who I am. My name is myself.'

'You mean, if you were called something else you'd be a different person? If you were called William or – Honorius, say, all that makes you Adrian would be as nothing?'

'No, but if I were called William I would *be* William – William would be me.'

'Then, if you were called William we would be the same person?'

'It's time to pack up here,' Adrian said. 'Let's be going to our dinners. You'd be a mutton-head whatever you were called.'

Five

Adrian and Will sat on the churchyard wall and watched the company straggling through the evening sunshine towards them. It seemed to Adrian that from his earlier misgiving that they would never be able to find enough players, there were far more people approaching than he recalled summoning.

Hugh was there already, scanning the crowd with pursy disapproval. Just coming in at the gate were the schoolboys, Giles, Henry, Philip and Anthony, and Gilbert trailing sulkily behind them. Then came Adam of Muscovy with David the harper alongside, inseparable, like an old married couple. No one grudged the portion of the council's nine and sevenpence that was maintaining them at the Bear for the sake of Adam's expertise. None doubted Adam's expertise. Only an expert could talk so hard and so fast, even if no one was very sure of what he was talking about. Once lubricated he could keep going for hours.

At the rear a second contingent from the Bear was just coming into view along the river path: Wat the plasterer and his merry men. Adrian had not asked any other workmen to join the company, first assuming that they would not be interested and then, having seen what Will was writing, doubting if they would be able to get their tongues around the words he was setting down for his characters. Wat had no such doubts. From having enlisted, Adrian suspected, because he knew they did not want him to, he had set about recruiting a band of fellow enthusiasts, all of them in the building trades; tilers, thatchers, joiners and bricklayers; his own private army. One thing Adrian was sure of, he dared not turn them away after they had left their ale to come to this first rehearsal, but what was he to do with them all?

No, they had not left their ale. As they came closer he saw that several of them carried jugs. Please God, if they got drunk let them be happy drunks, not surly drunks or falling-down drunks. Already he saw factions developing, workmen versus schoolboys with himself and Will caught in the middle. Will, he was alarmed to see, was still writing, marking up the pages with a bit of pointed lead.

Last of all, some way behind Wat's gang, came Stephen Thacker, Will's fellow-apprentice in the glove shop. Beside him, arguing violently, although they were too far away for him to hear anything, was Adrian's own Katherine, bent on talking Stephen out of taking part having failed to make any headway with Adrian. Adrian lowered his eyes. I must not let this sway my judgement when I am directing Stephen, he told himself piously, and looked up in time to see Katherine take a swing at Stephen's head and flounce away again.

By now the bulk of the company had settled around them. Will looked at them and they gazed back expectantly.

'Are you going to address them or shall I?' he said.

'You start,' Adrian said cravenly. He did not want to be the one who explained the play; it might have changed out of all recognition since Saturday.

'Are we all here?' Will said.

'Dunno. How many are we supposed to be?' someone called out.

'We're all here,' Adrian said. Stephen was just sitting down, rubbing his ear. 'All here and more than we need.'

'I'll call out the parts—'

'Parts of what?' The voice came again, from the direction of Wat's cohort.

'This is a play,' Adrian said. 'You know that. The persons in the play are called parts.'

'Don't they have names?'

'Yes; each part has a name,' Will said. 'I'll start with the naming of parts.'

'Never mind that,' Wat shouted. 'What's it about, this play? Or haven't you made your mind up about that, yet?'

Little do you know . . . Adrian thought. Will, scowling, was heaving himself off the wall, fists clenched.

Adam of Muscovy rose magisterially. 'Masters, be patient.' They all shut up. This was the expert. 'We can't have everything all at once. The way it's done is this. First William here tells us the matter of the play, that is, what it is about and what befalls, and then he calls out who shall take each part and play it. Now, in a company where men play many parts, the book-holder knows who will do well in one part above another, who will make a good priest or a clown, or a virtuous maiden . . .' a chorus of catcalls broke out at the idea of a virtuous maiden being found thereabouts '. . . and he needs not spend time deciding who is fittest.'

He was getting into his stride. How were they going to break in? The man seemed to breath in even as he breathed out.

'But you are new to this calling; when the play is told we must hear people speak and see them play so that we know who fits each part best. Sometimes those with the finest voices act like a side of beef swinging in the breeze.'

Adrian tried not to look at Giles Butcher, he of the maidenly voice and physique like a bull-calf. If he and Will ever went head to head it would be like watching two young neats vying for the same heifer.

'So, Will, tell us your play.' Equal to the occasion, Adam was playing a part already, master of ceremonies.

Will climbed back on to the wall. 'This is the tragedy of Honorius and Francisco, sons of the Duke of Hungary.'

'No Duke ever went hungry,' Stephen said.

'No Dukes at all since Norfolk lost his head,' Philip chimed in. Watch out for the Thacker brothers, Adrian warned himself. They may not be twins but they look out for each other, and that swine Stephen's after my girl.

'Hun-ga-ry,' Will said. 'It's a foreign country. The Duke is getting old and wants to know which of the brothers should be his heir.'

'The oldest!' Richard the bricklayer shouted. 'That's only fair and right.'

'They're twins —'

'Even one twin has to be born before the other,' Anthony said, reasonably, 'even Jacob and Esau, and they came out fighting.'

'Look, all this is explained. When the play begins, two gentlemen come on and tell each other that the brothers were so alike in the cradle that none could tell which was which.'

'They aren't alike now, then?'

'No,' Adrian said, improvising rapidly, 'because if they were we would have to find twins to play them.'

'Why do these gentlemen have to tell each other?' Wat asked. 'Don't they know already?'

'It's a device,' Will said. 'Of course they know all this but the audience won't. It's really the audience that's being told.'

'Then why have you got people talking to *each other*? Why doesn't one gentleman step up and tell the people to their faces?'

'It works better this way,' Will said, a shade desperately, 'really it does. One gentleman, Fabio, is lately come to Court and the other gentleman, Valentine, is explaining how things stand. Then Francisco and his wife come in and greet both gentlemen and then enter Honorius and his wife—'

'Where are all these people coming *from*?'

'What do you mean?'

'Why do they all come in one after the other?'

'This is a court, not a cottage. Everybody doesn't live in one room.'

'Masters!' Adam broke in again. 'If we go on like this it will be time to break fast before Will has even told us the play. You have all seen plays yourselves, put on by the London companies. Think back. Did you keep calling out whys and wherefores or did you just stand and watch and listen and believe everything as it fell out before you? Didn't you stand in the yard of the Swan in Bridge Street, in Stratford town, in the County of

Warwick, beside Avon River, in England, under an English sky, in English weather, and yet believed that you were in France, or Illyria, or Tartary, in broiling heat or icy waste? Before your eyes Englishmen walked on boards of English oak with the windows and walls of the inn behind them, and yet you saw old Romans, Spaniards, Bohemians, and you heard English speech on English tongues and yet understood that these men spoke a foreign language. Now, because it is your own selves who will be treading the boards you can not trust an audience to do the same for you and you can not trust yourselves to make it happen.'

'That's right, lads. Shut up!' Wat roared, and the restive group fell silent again.

'The way of it is this,' Will said; 'after the sons and their wives come in the Duke enters with *his* wife and speaks a speech explaining that because he feels old age coming upon him he wishes his sons to help him rule the kingdom—'

'Isn't it a Dukedom?'

'Belt up!'

'Dukedom,' Will said, making a hasty alteration with the lead point. 'And he announces it to everyone—'

'That's seven, including wives, by my count.'

'He speaks to the audience as if they were his court. He says he prays that Honorius and Francisco will rule wisely and if they ever come across anything that they can not handle they'll come to him for advice. Meanwhile, he says, he wishes to spend time away from the cares of state with his Duchess who is, by happy fortune, with child again.'

'Wait about,' Richard said. He was counting on his fingers. 'How old are these twins? You make them sound like grown men and yet here's their mother in the family way again.'

'Maybe their mother died in childbed and the Duke has a new young wife,' Stephen suggested.

'My mother bore her first child two-and-twenty years ago,' Will said, 'and in a month or less we shall see her delivered again, if God pleases,' he added fervently.

'Or perhaps this hungry Duchess is like Sarah the wife of Abraham, you know: "Abraham and Sarah were old and well stricken in age; and it ceased to be with Sarah after the manner of women." But the Lord sent her a son, Isaac. She was *ninety*,' Giles said, with awe.

'That was in marvellous olden times,' Stephen told him. 'How many women do you know who live to be ninety, let alone bear sons?'

'For sweet Christ's sake!' Will exploded. 'We've been here half an hour and I'm still on page two. Hear me out, then tell me what you think.

'These are two grown men, these brothers, *young* grown men.' The lead point was busy again. 'Now, the Duchess and the brothers and their wives all go out with Fabio, the gentleman, and the Duke confides in Valentine, the *other* gentleman, who is his friend, that although in truth he wishes to take a smaller part in the affairs of state, he also has a stratagem. Since no one knows which brother is the elder, he wants to see which of them rules more wisely before deciding which of them shall be his heir.'

'Why can't they just go on ruling wisely together?' Anthony called out.

'That's exactly what Valentine says. And the Duke replies that he's thought of that but other times it's been tried there's been a fatal falling out, like Romulus and Remus or Ferrex and Porrex. So, he says, Honorius shall rule the north of the king— dukedom, and Francisco shall rule the south, and whichever turns out best shall rule the whole thereafter. He himself favours Francisco, but his wife, he says, looks more loving on Honorius.'

'Jacob and Esau; same thing; told you,' Anthony murmured.

'Then Valentine tells Fabio of the Duke's plan, in good faith, but Fabio is a friend to Francisco and discloses—'

'Can't you just speed it up a bit?' Hugh pleaded. 'You don't need to tell us who says what and when.'

'Oh, all right. Well, we see the brothers ruling, and at their ease with their wives, and with their father, and the Duke goes on thinking that Francisco is the best choice as heir, but the rest of us, the audience, can see that he is not a true son and brother. And Francisco discovers the stratagem and plots to make his brother seem a villain. Then Honorius finds out and they quarrel and Francisco is killed. And – and other things happen and Honorius is sent into exile and the ghost of his brother follows him.'

'Who rules the Dukedom, then?' Philip said.

'Ah, the Duchess is with child, remember. Adrian thought of that,' Will said, scrupulously. 'At the end she is safely delivered of a son and everyone dances a gay galliard to celebrate the joyful news.'

'Is that *it*?' Henry Fielden, who had kept quiet so far, spoke up, glaring all the while somewhere to the left of Will's head.

'What do you mean, is that it? What more do you want?'

'It's just a lot of talking.'

'A murder, a ghost – a lot of talking? I can only write what people will say, and their entrances and exits. You, the players, will make them live.'

'What is an exit?' Richard said.

'It's Latin,' Henry said. 'It means a going-out.'

'Why doesn't he say so, then?'

'Do you want to know the parts you will play?' Adrian said. He was supposed to be directing this lot, it was time to assert his authority, or at least to remind them that he was there.

'That's why we're here, isn't it?'

'Yes, it is.' Not that anyone would think so. 'When you know who you are to play we'll meet again and you will be given your words to learn.'

'Adam said we must be heard and watched—'

'I've *been* watching you,' Adrian said.

'How if we can't read?'

'Then someone who can read will say your words aloud to you until you have them by heart. We won't give a long part to anyone who finds it hard—'

'Oh, I see,' Wat said. 'The best parts will go to the great schoolboys.'

'No, that's not the way of it at all,' Will said. 'There are four women in this play.'

'Oh, yes, that's all *we're* good for,' Philip said, croaking and fluting by turns.

'Be reasonable,' Adrian said. 'Wat could never play a woman, for instance.'

'Ho, couldn't I?' Wat broke into a quavering falsetto. 'Here comes I, the Duchess of Hungaree.'

'You would be wasted as the Duchess,' Will said.

'Then who am I to play?'

'We'll tell you in the order that you come on, the men, then the women,' Adrian said. 'First, Valentine, a gentleman. That will be your part, Anthony Stone.'

Anthony looked relieved. 'I'm not a woman, then?'

'Not while you have a stone to your name!' Wat

bawled, and the private army fell about laughing. Anthony blushed. Wat was emboldened.

'Why then, *do* you have only one stone?'

'Fabio!' Silence fell again, slowly. 'Philip Thacker.'

Philip turned a darker red than Anthony. 'Has Fabio much to say?'

'Very little, that's why we thought of you,' Will said with a staggering lack of tact.

'Your voice is settling down,' Adrian said, gently. 'It may be altogether broken by Whitsun.'

'What happens at Whitsun?' This was Matt the thatcher, one of Wat's party.

'The play, man; we're to do it at Whitsun,' Wat explained.

'We have asked Adam of Muscovy to play the part of the Duke,' Adrian said. 'The Duke has many long speeches and Adam is the best among us at that. Francisco is to be played by Hugh Burnet.'

'That was when Francisco was Arcturus the good brother,' Hugh said. 'This Francisco is not so good—'

'No, but a lot more interesting,' Will said. 'Barnard, servant to Francisco.'

'To be played by Richard Fisher.'

'Is that a long part?'

'Not in words.'

'True, you need not look for his long part in his mouth;' Wat again.

'Tobias, servant to Honorius, to be played by George Wainwright.'

George, another of Wat's gang, waved an enthusiastic arm. 'And I can read.'

'Then you can help teach the others. Ralph, a clown. That will be you, Wat.'

'Me play a clown, to be mocked and jeered at?' Wat was half-way to his feet.

'Not that kind of a clown,' Adrian said. 'He is servant to the Duke. Ralph is full of wit and mocks everyone else.'

'Oh, all right. I'll enjoy that.'

'That is all the men. Now, the women . . .'

The company manifested collective unease. Those who had no part yet looked covertly at each other.

'Henry Fielden, you will be the Duchess of Hungary. Stephen Thacker, you will be wife to Francisco,' Adrian said, rapidly, allowing no time for dissent. Let's see how Mistress Page fancies you now, my lady, he addressed Stephen, silently. 'Gilbert Shakespeare, you are wife to Honorius, and Giles Butcher, a gentlewoman attending upon the Duchess.' The Duchess and her lady-in-waiting, being of mature years, could be well covered up with wimples, to hide Henry's squint and Giles's flat nose.

'I play a woman?' Giles said, piteously.

'You have the voice for it,' Will said, 'if not the figure.'

Adam intervened. 'Forgive me if I missed something, but who is to play Honorius? It is his tragedy after all.'

'Adrian,' Will said.

'*What?* I can't play *any* part and direct it as well. You'll have to do it.'

'I didn't write it for me.'

'You're the only one left,' Adrian hissed, 'unless you want the part to go to Jakey the gravedigger or Matt the thatcher who has a wry neck since he fell off the tithe barn last year.'

'I'm not playing wife to my own brother,' Gilbert said.

'You needn't worry. There's no kissing in it.'

'We'll decide on this later,' Adrian said. 'We can resolve it between ourselves.'

'Why do I have to play a woman when Anthony here is to be a gentleman?'

'It's all in the voice,' Will said. 'If there were any natural justice you could play a raging tyrant, but God has given you the voice of a nightingale.'

'Aren't there any parts that don't speak at all?'

'There'd better be,' Wat said, 'because there are fellows here who've given up their evening to come along and now they have nothing to do.'

'How many?'

The remainder of Wat's army raised their hands. Adrian counted five including Jakey the gravedigger and Matt the wry-necked thatcher who, head cocked, seemed to be permanently on the alert for a call from above.

'Just enough,' Will said, thinking at speed. 'This play happens in great houses, there will be servants and courtiers who may cry "Aye!" and "Shame!" and suchlike things.'

'You should be able to manage that,' Wat said, clouting Jakey on the shoulder.

'And I can play my pipe for the galliard dance,' Jakey offered.

'It's a dance of rejoicing,' Adrian said, seeing his worst fears coming to pass. 'Your pipe does not make a joyful noise, Jakey, with all respect. It conjures up most mournful anguish.'

'Then he can play at the funeral,' Wat said.

'Is there to be a funeral?' Jakey said. 'Happen I can dig the grave.'

'There is no funeral.'

'Well, there ought to be,' Richard said. 'Francisco is slain by his brother. What are they going to do with the corpse; leave it lying around for anyone to trip over?'

'Nay, it will stink,' Jakey said.

'There is no body, Jakey,' Adrian explained. 'This is all in show. Francisco is to be played by Hugh here. Hugh is not going to die, is he? He will be seeming dead, that's all. Servants will bear away the corpse—'

'No,' Will cut in. 'Honorius drags it off-stage by the heels and says he will bury it privily.'

'Perhaps, when Francisco's death is discovered then the piper may play a lament,' Adam suggested. 'But for the dance we must have a pipe-and-tabor man.'

'And I will play my harp at the burying,' David said. As far as anyone knew he had not spoken for days. 'I'll play my harp and speed his soul to heaven.'

'This man will not be going to heaven, perhaps, but lie in the grave till the crack of doom,' Hugh said, earnestly. 'The living can not intercede for the dead. We were in error when we were told that prayers and masses could deliver a soul from purgatory.'

'Someone sit on his head.'

'No, but he's right,' Henry said. 'If his ghost walks, he cannot be in heaven.'

'These are old heathens,' Will shouted. 'They do not know what we know. They do not sit in church to hear homilies and sermons. They did not go to the Grammar School. They were benighted!'

On cue, the sun went down.

'Time to be moving, boys, if our young masters are done with discussing the life to come.' Wat was on his feet. 'This life's enough to be going on with, to my mind. Back to the Bear!'

Adrian, who had been wondering how to bring the

proceedings to an orderly close, watched as the army arose and followed Wat to the gate. *They* had all had a good time at any rate. The schoolboys were next. He noticed that a schism had occurred among them. Gilbert, Henry and Giles, three bruisers condemned by their voices to play gentle ladies, were cold-shouldering Anthony and Philip, particularly Anthony who would have made some man a lovely wife and had got away with the part of Valentine.

He had several doubts about Philip. He might not have much to say but he was the first to say anything:

> 'How now, friend Valentine, tell me how things
>   stand
> Between our lord the Duke and his two sons.'

Having heard him speak out in company he realized that although Philip would in truth have sounded unconvincing as a woman, he was going to sound pretty ludicrous as a man. And Wat had a point when he complained that all the best parts had gone to the schoolboys. In fact it was that the most impressive parts had gone to the people he and Will had judged most able to speak them.

They could have been wrong. Wat himself had a perfectly good voice and considerable presence, more presence than Philip, for a start. Perhaps when things got under way they could try a little discreet shuffling around, as Adam had assumed they would.

'Are we for the Bear?' Hugh said. The three of them were the only ones left in the darkling churchyard, apart from Adam of Muscovy who was gently guiding David the harper to the gate.

'What are we going to do about *him*?' Adrian said quietly, to Will. 'He thinks he can play again.'

'He thinks so now. Will he in a week's time, or even tomorrow?'

'Perhaps we can find him an unstrung harp and let him fumble at it in dumb show. I wouldn't hurt him for the world. We owe him for Adam.'

'And let us pray that Adam stays in his humour till Whitsun,' Will said. 'Doesn't it seem to you that our Davy is sinking fast? What shall we do if Adam sinks with him?'

Six

What had become of the two fine capons no one liked to ask, but their skins were now stretching over twin frames in the shop. Dorcas's mortal envelope, sadly chewed up where they had experimented with various threads and stitches, lay shrivelled on a bench. Her feet had left the premises. Dick had made the mistake of taking them to school where he had used them for tweaking people's ears. He had returned one dinner time sore and snivelling, and without the feet.

'Serves you right,' Joan said heartlessly, 'for serving poor Dorcas so.'

'Dumb creatures have no souls. It's foolish to name them and love them,' Mother said, wearied by the endless bickering caused by the hen's untimely death, especially since Molly, the one that they'd marked for martyrdom, had lately died of natural causes. 'God made them for our benefit like – like the cabbages in the garden. You don't name them Mary and Jane Cabbage and weep when we eat them. You don't give names to the *eggs*, do you?'

Will recalled his conversation with Adrian about names. A name was a man's self, his essence, perhaps his very soul. Until baptized and named a babe was held to have no soul, either. So what purpose was there in naming brute beasts — apart from the fact that it came naturally to do it, foolish or not. Every dog and cat had a name, every horse and cow. People seemed to call a halt when it came to naming sheep, but poor Joan had named her hens. And yet it was not for their non-existent souls she wept but the loss of what seemed to be their love.

Perhaps when the baby arrived she would find a new object for her affections, which would be a poor look-out for Dick, already convinced that nobody loved him. Gilbert had overheard him talking to himself in the cubby-hole under the stairs, muttering darkly of running away and taking a ship to London and becoming a felon.

'Bless us,' Mother said, 'why does he want to become a felon?'

'He thinks it's some kind of a soldier,' Gilbert said. 'I told him felons were hanged and he could as easily be hanged here in Stratford if he wanted, and save himself the bother of running away.'

Will ate his dinner standing in the kitchen, bread, ale, cold meat; gobbling it down alongside Gilbert who was in no hurry to get back to school.

'What's your rush?' Gilbert said, sourly.

'I have the copying to do when work's over. So do you.'

'Don't I do enough copying all day?'

'I know it's a burden, but it will soon be done. You write the finest hand of all of us. Do you like it?'

'Do I like copying? Didn't I just say . . . ?'

'No.' Will was anxious. 'The play. Do you think it's good?'

'Well, I may do when I see it all together, but you've got me copying Honorius's part and his cues. I don't know why he does what he does because I don't know what anyone else does.'

'Would you rather we copied out the play whole for every man to read?'

'No, I wouldn't, we'd be at it till Lammas. But it would make more sense,' Gilbert said. 'First Honorius thinks noble thoughts and speaks well of his brother and then out he comes and calls him a dissembling knave, a whitewashed tomb – and that's *before* he kills him.'

'Whited sepulchre – it's from Holy Writ. A figure of speech.'

'His speech is full of figures.'

'You don't like it, then.'

'I'll like it better when I've finished with it. And when I've seen what *I* have got to say—'

'You can copy your own part too, Gilbert. It will help you to remember it.'

'Thanks very much. And Will, I meant it. If you're to play Honorius I *won't* play your wife.'

'You're as bad as Wat and his friends. It won't be *my* wife. It's only in the play.'

'He – Honorius – calls her sweeting and duck. Would I have to say that to you?'

'It wouldn't *be* me. I'd be Honorius. Anyway, I don't much want to play Honorius. Adrian can do it.'

'How do you know he can act?'

'I don't know that any of us can act. It won't be like it is in school, standing still, with gestures.'

'So it may turn out that Wat and Richard and George Wainwright are better than us. Even Jakey might be.'

'I draw the line at Jakey,' Will said, 'but you may be right.'

'I'll tell you what,' Gilbert said, 'I think your words are too clever by half. That old Glovers' Play you started with, it was plain English that anyone could understand. It's one thing when the audience can't understand what's being said, but when the players can't either, you're in trouble. You may have to smooth it out.'

He took a last heel of bread to sustain him on the walk back to school and went out. Will watched him go despondently, wiped his hands and went into the shop. As spring drew on trade was picking up a little. As well as the dreaded chicken-skin gloves Peter Starling had ordered fancy leather pairs for all the guests, and there was another wedding coming up, less lavish but still a substantial order. Spring turned people's thoughts to love; understandings might become betrothals; tokens would be exchanged, gloves, pretty belts, purses.

John Shakespeare was cheering up along with the weather. He still steered clear of the other burgesses but he was less morose than he had been. Will envied the easy friendship between Adrian and his father. True, Adrian was older, but only by three years, and Master Croft was younger, by perhaps ten. It ought not to make that much difference, but Adrian reported that he had proposed to his father, half in jest, that he should play the Duke of Hungary. Will dared not imagine what kind of a response he would have got if he had laid a similar proposition before his father. He had tentatively tried to recruit Martin the journeyman. Martin had not even bothered to look up from his bench. Instead he raised his fingers in a derisive gesture. 'Dream on.'

But they had Adam, so long as Adam's humour held, and in truth it seemed more stable now. The spurts and gushes of words had become a steady flow that could be stanched and diverted with questions and answers. But there was poor Davy to worry about, visibly ailing, following strange paths through his head that led him to unknown halls and manors where he played his harp and sang his songs; to ruined monasteries where the brothers still kept open house for the travelling poor. He continued to believe that when he and Adam moved on, his way might bring him at last to a house of God where he would end his days in the faith that had been taken from him. By the few things he had said, Will understood that in David's creed his soul would indeed go to purgatory and, if his sins were heavy enough, his perturbed spirit would walk the earth, whatever Hugh and his kind might say to the contrary.

Conversation was muted at the Bear that night. The longest shovelboard in Warwickshire stood empty, groats remained in purses and the fireside corner where Adam held court was vacant.

Adrian came in late after an evening's copying, and found Will sitting alone by the window. Wat and his gang were subdued. After a while Adam joined them. All heads turned in his direction. Will and Adrian looked at one another. They were both ashamedly consumed by the same thought; if David died what effect was this going to have on Adam's fluid humours? By his own reckoning he ought to be merry until Michaelmas, but what humour had he been in when he made that reckoning?

'Sleeping,' Adam said, before they could ask. 'As peaceful as a child. No grief, no pain.'

'What does he die of?' Will said. Adrian hoped he would leave it at that. Will, with his insatiable curiosity, his voracious appetite for facts, was likely to demand a list of symptoms, as if he were compiling a mental catalogue of all that made a man human so that he could consult it at a later date, along with his information on the plastering, baking and weaving trades, none of which was his business. Still, eventually, the trade of dying was one that they would all have to master.

'He dies of old age; a little sorrow and much confusion,' Adam said. 'Last night as I sat by him he talked of a bed of ashes, and how he might breathe his last with the holy oil upon him and the Host upon his tongue, and the sound of the brothers' singing in his ears.'

'A bed of ashes?' Wat said. 'He wants to die in the fireplace?'

'No, this is the old way, as he must have heard when he was young. Those in Holy Orders, when they knew the end was near, would have a bed of ashes strewn on the floor and themselves laid upon it as a sign that the mortal body was only dust and ashes for from dust was man made by God in the beginning.'

'Should we call the Parson to give him the Sacrament?' Wat said.

'He talks of the mass . . . extreme unction.'

'Parson would understand,' Wat said. 'It's not like our poor Davy is a heretic. He's just gone back a way – a long way – in his wits.'

'He's not so wandering that he doesn't know he's dying,' Adam said. 'But he doesn't suffer bodily. He's going easily, it might be days.'

'He should confess, and soon,' Will said. 'You know the story of the knight who put off confessing until he was well again, and demons tore out his vitals with ploughshares and carried him off to hell.'

'Do you dare to say David has such sins on his conscience?' Adam looked as near angry as they had ever seen him.

'No, but if I know the story it's more than likely that he does. We don't want him to die in fear for his soul.'

'Promise him masses,' Adrian said. 'It can do no harm.'

'Lie to a dying man?'

'To let him die easy.' He was relieved that puritanical Hugh was not there to make heresy of kind men's good intentions.

'My father had the Glovers' Play from a man who died wanting a priest,' Will said. 'If it weren't for him we'd none of us be here now, with David of our company.'

'I'd pray for his soul,' Wat said. 'If it's true that it can do no good, it can do no ill, neither.'

'He fears to die in his sleep, unready,' Adam said, 'but it seems to me it would be the kindest way.'

'Call on us when the time comes,' Wat said. 'Day or night, he'll go with his friends about him.'

'Wat's not such a clod when you get to know him,' Adrian said, on the way home.

'I never did think he was a clod, I just came up at him on the wrong side. He has a fine voice.'

'Are you thinking what I'm thinking?' Adrian said.

'What, that he's wasted as a clown? I don't know . . . he'll make an excellent clown if he can remember the words; but he'd make an excellent Fabio, too.'

'Fabio's a gentleman.'

'Only because I wrote him so,' Will said. 'He might be a shepherd.'

'Or a plasterer, come to that. Why would Valentine be sharing court secrets with a shepherd?'

'Or an honest yeoman, up from the country?'

'Could we swap them round? Let Philip play the clown.'

'Well, for God's sake, every time he opens his mouth people start to laugh. He sounds like a ram being gelded.'

'He doesn't really want to play any part at all,' Adrian said, 'but if we take Fabio away from him and give it to Wat he'll die of shame. And never mind Fabio, who's to play Honorius?'

'Why, you are,' Will said. 'Didn't we agree?'

'I can't, I told you. Don't sound so innocent. How can I direct sixteen players if I'm to be one of them? You've seen how they argue, half of them will need every word explained. Honorius has the greatest part of all. You'll have to do it.'

'I can't learn all that.'

'Then cut it down. You wrote it, you can shorten it.'

'Gilbert will never forgive me. He's just done copying it.'

'Then let Adam of Muscovy play Honorius and you be the Duke. I know he has long speeches but he doesn't have all that many, and anyway, you wrote them too. Adam won't mind how great or small a part he gets.'

'But the Duke is an old man. Adam must be five-and-thirty at least. How can I play his father?'

'We can feign old age. You may wear a beard of sheep's wool and hide your own hair under a great wide hat. We can hang more wool around the crown to give you white hairs.'

'Wool doesn't look like hair.'

'From a distance – if we wash it well and comb it out. It would pass for *your* hair, anyway. When you get on in years your hair will probably look just like sheep's wool – it's springy enough.'

Will let the insult pass. 'I can ask Joan to see about the wool, if she ever speaks to me again. By Christ, that hen sits heavy on my soul,' he said. 'But don't you want to be in the play? Do you mislike it?'

'No, it's well pleasing, but if I'm to direct it I must be out at the front to see what everyone is doing. I can't always be turning round and looking backwards.'

'It's not too long?'

'It's as long as it needs to be.'

'Not too many great speeches?'

'No . . . there are a lot, but they don't all come together.'

'Do you think it will please the people? When the Queen's Men or Essex's Men come to town no one knows who wrote the plays, nor cares, neither, but if they mislike this one they'll know who wrote it, right enough.'

'We need not say you wrote it – just announce that it was . . . *patched* by William Shakespeare.'

'There's not enough of it left to call it patched, it's all mine now except for the plot – two brothers who quarrel and one kills the other. I won't have it taken for another man's work.'

'But, the division of the kingdom – you took that from *Gorbuduc*.'

'They are my *words*.'

'You can't have it both ways,' Adrian said. 'Good or bad, either it's yours or it's not yours. Which will you mind more, being blamed if it displeases and everyone knows it's yours, or forfeiting the praise if it's good and people think someone else wrote it?'

Will was still mulling this over when they reached his door.

'Do you think it's good?' he said at last.

'I couldn't have written it,' Adrian said.

'That's not what I asked,' Will said. 'I dare say you couldn't have written it, and nor could Hugh, or Jakey, as far as that goes. But I did write it and I want to know, is it good?'

'Parts of it are excellent,' Adrian said. 'It's not fair to ask me yet, Will. It looks very well on paper, but we won't know if it's a good play until our players play it.'

'Our players could turn *Gorbuduc* into *Gammer Gurton's Needle*.' Will spoke hollowly from the dark doorway. 'Listen, Adrian, we must start to rehearse as soon as maybe.'

'Before the parts are learned?'

'They'll be learned all the sooner on the hoof. Gilbert was complaining that he could make no sense of the parts he copied without knowing the rest, and he didn't have time to read the rest in between the cues. When people realize that they are talking to each other and not just saying words, they will find it easy to remember.'

'Then I'll tell you something. We must fix on the parts before people start learning them because they'll never be unlearned. We *must* do something about

Philip Thacker. I'll call a rehearsal for Sunday, after evensong.'

'Where?'

'In the churchyard,' Adrian said. 'At least that will ensure that everybody's there. We can be first out of the church and waylay the others as they come by.'

Will went quietly in. Adrian walked the short distance home with a weight on his shoulders, mentally moving his men around like pieces on a chess board, back, forwards, sideways, diagonal. How to persuade Philip that he did not want to play Fabio without taking the part bodily from him and giving it to Wat? Perhaps brother Stephen could lean on him – after Will had leaned on Stephen. Adrian himself might lean too hard. Before the play had driven her from him, he had been going to ask Will to make Katherine a pair of gloves to give as a token on May Day, with perhaps a line or two of verse, hinting at his devotion if not actually declaring it. Stephen, God rot him, could make all the gloves he wanted. Katherine would never have cold hands with Stephen around.

Probably Wat would not want to play Fabio in any case. The plasterer had been pleased with the part of Ralph and Ralph was a clever clown, not a clodpoll. People should laugh at what he said, not at the way he said it. Will had a good voice, but could he handle Honorius and if he did, would the others then complain that he had written the best part for himself? Better he played the Duke.

One thing Adrian was determined on: he would direct the players. If nothing more, it would keep him out of the play.

Seven

David lingered, but even while he lived his death cast a long shadow. Will and Adrian fell in with Adam as they walked to church.

'He's easy in his mind,' Adam said. 'He has received the Sacrament and confessed to the Parson, thinking him to be a priest and the Parson did not take affront when Davy begged him to pray for his soul.'

'There'll be prayers for his soul,' Adrian said, 'as you heard the other evening.'

'And how is it with you, Adam?' Will said, voicing what they were both thinking, but Adrian had not the nerve to utter. 'Are you easy in your mind?'

'I know what you're afraid of,' Adam said, without rancour, 'that were I in my heavy fit I might run mad with sorrow. No. It is not in that wise. It would take less than a friend's death to move me to despair; in truth, I should be in such despair already that a friend's death would not move me at all. You can not know how it is unless you have been in that dark place yourself, for a man is all alone in it. Friends come by and seek to cheer him with ale and song and good company; women console and offer themselves for very pity's sake, and yet it is as if he sits in a room of glass walls, where it is dark and silent. Outside, the sun shines, the birds sing, flowers bloom, and a man can see it all, he can see his friends, but they are no more than shadows on the glass, their voices come from far off and mean nothing. A woman may lie down beside him in his bed, but she will be a shadow, whatever they may do together. Truth, if Davy had died while I was in my room of glass I should no more have noticed his passing than if a bird had flown across the panes. For his sake, I am glad to be in this present humour for I shall be able to mourn him properly and be fitly sorry to lose him.

'But he is old, he is ready to go in the fullness of his years. I shall not mourn overmuch. He must have harped at many a wake in his youth, I think he would like us to speed him on his way with a little ale and song. In short, young William, I shall not be knocked sideways with grief and unable to play in your play.'

'That's good to hear,' Adrian said. They were nearing the church porch and he had a seed to plant in Adam's fertile mind. 'Are you set on playing the Duke of Hungary?'

'Give me any part you choose and I'll play it,' Adam said, expansively. 'I'll play the Duchess if you like. Before now I've doubled as the King and Queen of Denmark. There was some slight confusion when they both came on at once.'

He went ahead leaving them less reassured than they had hoped or he had intended. How slight a confusion could it have been when the same player appeared on stage in two parts at once? What kind of a play was it where a man could come on as two people at the same time and cause only a slight confusion?

Neither of them paid a great deal of attention during the service. Will had the playbook with him and, Adrian was dismayed to see, was out with the lead point again. Every alteration he made would have to be duplicated on the relevant part.

Adrian sat with his father. The Shakespeare pew was depleted; John Shakespeare rarely came to church these days and his wife was awaiting her confinement. Will reported that there had been early pains and so no one was taking any chances. What happened if you were to give birth in church? It would be a good start in life for the baby, no doubt, but a woman would want to be in her own house, not God's. Will sat at one end of the pew, Joan at the other, Gilbert and Dick between them. Joan was a pretty girl, all girls were pretty. What a shame women could not be players; would it be so very wrong if they were? It would make his life a lot easier if women could be played by women. There must be a proscription in Holy Writ, not one of the Ten Commandments but something obscure in the Book of Leviticus.

Quite apart from the benefits of realism it would be a diversion to have comely girls on stage from time to time, to sing and dance, perhaps, or exchange saucy banter with clowns . . . a whole line of pretty maidens dancing and singing . . . not that there would be any place for that in Will's heavy tragedy where the leaven was distributed sparingly in the form of Ralph and the two servants. They must get a dance or two in somewhere.

What was he going to do about Philip? The Thacker brothers were sitting several rows in front of him. Philip, destined for University and the Law, would be leaving school this summer; Stephen, no intellectual, had been hauled out early and indentured to Will's father.

Stephen was casting sidelong glances at Katherine Page, as Adrian could tell by her studied indifference from the far side of the aisle. Philip, head drooping on that too-thin neck, was not attending to the homily either. Perhaps he was getting his schoolwork by heart, ready for tomorrow.

When evensong ended Adrian was out of the pew almost before the Benediction was over.

'A little less haste,' his father said. 'The rehearsal can not begin without you.'

'It can get out of hand without me,' Adrian said,

slowing down but not stopping. 'Will and I need to be at the door to catch our players as they come out.'

'Will's there already,' Robert Croft said. 'He moves even faster than you. Go on then, Adrian. Are you afraid you'll lose them otherwise?'

'A few are having second thoughts,' Adrian said. 'The ones who are to play women.' He saw Stephen streak past to be intercepted by Will in the porch. Philip followed more slowly, hobbling.

'What ails you?' Adrian said, hit by the base suspicion that Philip was feigning infirmity. A real infirmity would be an answer to his prayers but he did not want the burden of knowing that he had prayed for it.

'I trod on a nail,' Philip said. 'A great rusting thing that caught me under the instep. It went right through my shoe.'

'Into your flesh?'

'Mother put a bandage on it. It didn't hurt so much this afternoon, but sitting in church I felt it swelling up.'

His voice, which had stayed low till then, soared climactically on the last word. What a shame it was only his foot, Adrian thought. That would not prevent him from speaking.

'It hurts passing bad,' Philip said. His face was pale and two trails of sweat dewed his face from the wings of his nose to the corners of his mouth. 'It's a long walk home.'

'Would you rather go now, and Stephen can bring your part to you?'

'If you like,' Philip said, listlessly. 'I'm not in the vein to study anything now.'

'Where's he going?' Will demanded at the door, seeing Philip limp by, out of reach.

'He's hurt his foot,' Adrian said.

'Too badly hurt to play Fabio?'

'He ran a nail into it, he says.'

'Then we must give the part to someone else until he recovers. By then, perhaps, he won't want it.'

'He certainly doesn't want it now,' Adrian said, filled with the same unholy hope, even as his conscience smote him. 'It's a good excuse, there's no shame in being unable to play. Then we can say it's too late to start again.'

Having come straight from the church the company was without ale this evening. Adrian assumed his perch on the wall; Will stood below him with the sheaf of parts and the playbook, but no one took any notice of their preliminary throat-clearing until Adam stood up and his mere presence silenced them.

'We give out the parts tonight,' Adrian said. 'Starting with those who speak first. Fabio.'

'That's our Philip,' Stephen said. 'He has a bad foot,' he explained to the others. 'He had to go home.'

'You take his part,' Will said.

'What, I play Fabio? He won't like that.'

'No, you take it *to* him. But you might study it yourself,' Adrian said. 'If Philip does not mend in time—'

'So I need not play wife to Francisco?' Stephen said. 'I can't be both at once.'

'Francisco's wife doesn't say much.'

'Didn't we think Wat for Fabio?' Will hissed.

'Best to keep it in the family – and kinder.'

'But Francisco's wife?' Stephen persisted.

'It's your true part, study it. Anyone can get it by heart later, if they need to.'

'You'd think Philip was already dead and buried,' Anthony observed.

'Valentine, that's you, Anthony,' Adrian said quickly. 'Here's your part. Duke of Hungary: Will's playing that.'

'I thought it was to be Adam,' Wat called out. 'You're a fine pair, promising us one thing and then taking it away and giving it to another.'

'Adam is to be Honorius,' Adrian said. 'He's best suited to it. Honorius has the most words to say.' He hurried on. 'Hugh, here's Francisco for you.'

'Adam's to play my *twin*?'

'You're the same height.' Adrian skimmed over other drawbacks. 'Richard Fisher, George Wainwright – Barnard and Tobias, servants to Francisco and Honorius.'

'These men say a great deal,' George said, doubtfully.

'No, it only seems so,' Will said. 'What you have written down there are your lines and the cues.'

'What are cues?'

'The cue is the last line spoken by the person who speaks before you.'

'So I must know the other man's words as well?'

'Yes, know them, not say them,' Adrian said. 'When you hear Honorius say, "It seems to me indeed it may be so," *you* come in and say, "My lord, the Duke your father bid me come—" Do you see?'

'Do I say that or does he?' Richard and George spoke together. Adrian foresaw problems.

'When you have studied your words you will know who says what and when.'

Richard had sized up his part rapidly. 'I have five inches and a quarter.'

'Yes, but can you read them?'

'Not I,' Richard said, contentedly.

'Who is going to help you study?'

'I'll do that,' George said. 'I'll tell them till he knows them.'

'Then, Richard, you had better let George have yours too—'

Richard clutched his part possessively. 'Are you saying I can't be trusted with it? I've a wife and children at home. I keep a pig. I do an honest day's work. Are you saying I can't be trusted with this here piece of paper?'

'You might forget what it is,' Will said.

'Why should I? I don't have any other pieces of paper at home. I shan't mistake it for a dish of onions. Look, if you're worried, get your pointy thing and put the letters of my name on it. I can't read words, but I know the letters of my name.'

'Wat!' Adrian said. 'Here's the part of Ralph for you.'

'On paper?' Wat lumbered to his feet and took the part. He examined it with exaggerated care, turning it all ways. 'I thought you'd be sending me to look at a wall.'

Will had forgotten their last exchange on the subject of reading. 'What are you talking about?'

'You told me that I read walls as well as you read books. I've been looking at that wall this last quarter-hour. I've got it by heart. Do you want to hear it?'

Adrian intervened. 'That's a good jest, Wat, but leave it out, will you? George, or one of us, will help you to study. With your quick wit you should find it easy.'

'Spread the honey good and thick,' Wat said, poking him in the chest. 'When you can spread plaster as good you can call me a quick wit.'

'Now the ladies,' Adrian said, writhing away from under Wat's finger. 'Henry, you're to be the Duchess, come up for your part. Gilbert, Stephen, Giles; the two wives and the gentlewoman.'

The boys rose and surged forward in a body, as though charging a lone sentry. Adrian slid off the wall before their impetus could tip him over it. No one, it appeared, was going to be able to cast doubts on their virility, even if they ended up in kirtles and farthingales.

'What about us?' Matt and Jakey and their friends were waving. 'What about we who are to cry "Aye" and "Shame"?'

Adam quelled them with a gesture. 'You do not need parts written out for that. You have only to know when you must speak, as in church when the Parson says, "O Lord, open Thou our lips," and the people answer, "And our mouths shall show forth Thy praise." '

'That is more words than "Aye" or "Shame",' Jakey complained.

'No, no,' Will said. 'Adam was but making a comparison. *You* do not say, "And our mouths shall show forth Thy praise," but he means that you have only to speak at certain times, which you will learn.'

George was already in trouble. 'How shall we say these words if we don't know what they mean? It says here, *Enter Uxor Honorii*. What is Uxor? Is it an angel?'

'It means his wife,' Hugh said. 'Wife of Honorius.'

'Why doesn't it say wife, then? Is her name Uxor? No, this cannot be. It is the same in Richard's part, *Enter*

Uxor Francisci. Master Will, it is not a good idea to have two ladies with the same name. People will not know which is which.'

'I don't know anyone called Uxor,' Matt the thatcher said. 'It's an ill name for a lady.'

'It's Latin,' Anthony said. Adrian noticed that the schoolboys were sniggering together over George's mistake. He immediately felt protective of his players. The true mistake was his and Will's.

'Have you written the directions in Latin?' Adam said. 'Why was that?'

Will had the grace to blush. 'I didn't think. That was how it was done in the Glovers' Play.'

'I suppose the copier was a learned man,' Adam said, 'writing it down for those who could read. I doubt the working men who played it ever saw it written down. Is there time to change it?'

'Not now,' Adrian said, aghast. 'It is on all the parts.'

Gilbert erupted. 'If you think I'm copying that lot out again—'

'Listen!' Will shouted. '*Enter* means enter in Latin *and* English. *Exit* means go out.'

'What means this other X?' George said. 'Exe-newt?'

'*Exeunt.* That means go out.'

'Then why . . . ?'

'*Exit* – one man goes out – or one woman. *Exeunt* – many men go out. *Exeunt omnes* – everyone goes out.

Uxor – wife. *Servus* – servant. There, now you know some Latin.' Will was quivering with exasperation.

'Listen, shortarse.' Wat towered over him. 'What call have you got to make game of these honest fellows because you've been to the Grammar School? Why did you write in Latin for them as can barely read their names in English?'

'I'm sorry,' Will said. 'Masters, it was an error, I shouldn't have done it.'

'I'm *not* going to copy—'

'Gilbert, shut up,' Adrian said. 'Ignore the directions for now. At the next rehearsal we'll change the words for those that need it, but you may find once we begin that you don't need the directions at all. You'll know them soon enough.'

'We hope,' Hugh muttered.

'Is this rehearsal over then?' Henry said. 'Are they all to be like this?'

'No, they aren't,' Adrian said. 'Next time we will begin to speak our parts and learn where we must walk, when to come in and out. Will Tuesday suit you all?'

'Two days? I can't learn all this in two days.'

'Thursday, then.'

'Not Thursday,' Will said. 'It's May Eve. You know how it is, everyone goes out to hear the nightingales and comes home with the lark.'

'And the Maypole. So Thursday night will see the

town empty. Shall you go out and help to bring home the May?'

'No, and neither will you. We have enough to do . . .'

'To my mind, May Revels are a heathenish practice and an affront to God,' Hugh said. 'There is much ill-doing in the woods on May Eve. The Scriptures tell us that those who go up into high places—'

'Why don't you go up into a high place and jump off?' someone growled.

'Wednesday, then,' Adrian cut in. He raised his voice. 'Did you all hear that?'

The company was already dribbling away. Wat sprang in front of them like an agile sheepdog. 'Listen up, my hearts! Adrian has something to say.' They all turned back.

'Wednesday; we'll meet here on Wednesday even and do it in action.'

'All of it?'

'We'll begin at the beginning and see how far we get.'

'That could be asking for trouble,' Henry said, but quietly. 'At this rate we'll get no farther than *Enter Fabio and Valentine*.'

As the company was bound for the Bear along the river path, Will and Adrian walked home with Hugh by way of the Old Town Street, and across the Rother Market, careful where they put their feet. Only heavy rain ever came near to cleansing the place and the stink of fearful beasts seemed to hover about it even on the six days between markets, as mist hung over the river.

They had parted from Hugh at the top of Scholars Lane.

'Will you be looked for at home?' Adrian said. 'Come and eat with us.'

Will was still cursing himself for the tactless mistake with the Latin. He did not want to face Gilbert's gibes. 'We need ale first. Let's stop at the Hart Royal.' And afterwards, he added to himself. With luck, by the time he got home everyone would have gone to bed.

The house was dark and silent when he returned, and the voice of the bellman, retreating down the street, told him that it was past nine o'clock. Curfew was long past, but as he headed for the stairs he saw a light flicker in the kitchen. His first thought, *fire*, made his heart jolt, but as he darted in he made it out to be a candle and, behind it, a pale phantasm, slowly pacing. Was he, who had so blithely arranged for a ghost to walk, about to see a very walking spirit? Oh, Jesus—

'Will?'

'Mother?'

She was wrapped in a white woollen shawl over her night rail.

'I took you for a felon.'

'I took you for a ghost.'

'Not yet, God willing.' She put down the candle on the table.

'What ails you? Is it the babe? Have the pains begun again?'

'No, don't fret.' She had borne seven children, four lived. She knew her trade. 'But I'm that aching and sore, lying down's no better than sitting. I was heaving and turning over so that I feared to wake your father, and he's snoring like a hedgehog in rut, so loud I couldn't sleep.'

They paused and listened deferentially to the rhythmic snorts and rumbles coming down from above.

'I'm easier on my feet,' she went on, 'walking about. Tomorrow I'll clean the bake oven.'

'So near your time? Joan can do that.'

'It's a good sign, Son.' She laughed quietly and propped herself against the table. 'Whenever a babe's due I get a terrible rage to clean and sweep and scrub, down on my knees. It helps to bring it on, I dare say. It was the same when Dick was born.'

'I remember that he took his time.'

'Three days. I was sure he'd be the last, if he wasn't the death of me first. You'd think it would get easier each time – some women are fortunate that way.'

'Not you?'

'It's God's will, I suppose.'

'How long did I take?'

'Only a day and a night, but you were a great lump. I thought you were twins, or a bull calf. This one ought to have a week to go, yet. All my babes are spring or autumn born.'

There was a shattering rasp from upstairs, a thump, then silence.

'He's turned on his side, thank God. I'll go up now and try to sleep myself.' She picked up the candle and moved towards the stairs, slow and heavy in the measure of a solemn dance. 'Bar the door, Son.'

He watched the candle and the shadows ascend.

'God send her a safe delivery,' he muttered, but he was already making mental notes. Suitably amended her revelations on childbirth might furnish a good speech for Henry, Duchess of Hungary.

Eight

It had been a good plan to hold rehearsals in the churchyard, too far from the town centre to attract the attentions of idle spectators who might come out of curiosity or a mere desire to mock. As word of the play spread through Stratford, people began to take an interest, which was encouraging, but Gilbert reported that the boys at school were also expressing an interest and that was less welcome, especially after it became known which parts their friends were playing. Anthony, cast as Valentine, got off lightly, and Gilbert himself, being a year or two younger than the others, was not worth ribbing, but Giles and Henry, in a desperate bid to cling to their dignity, had let it be understood without actually saying so, that they were to play lords or knights. When, inevitably, the truth leaked out, their downfall was all the crueller. Giles found posies on his form and was waylaid with offers to kiss his cherry lips, his lily cheeks, his dainty perfumed hand. Henry received an unforgiveable love-letter praising his eyes, 'blue orbs, the one that doth sidle up to the other like the amorous turtle.'

The two of them ambushed Will in Henley Street on the way home from one of his fruitless attempts to find a walnut big enough to contain the infamous chicken-skin gloves. He and Martin had been practising on Dorcas who was beginning to come apart, the skin splitting, the thread unravelling. She lay about the workshop like the remains of some alien creature brought back from Cathay by Sir John Mandeville, half glove, half chicken. Sir John had reported on a lamb that grew inside a gourd, blood, bones and flesh, perfectly edible.

'Listen, Shakespeare,' Giles said, an elbow across his throat. 'I will not play a woman and that's final.' Henry shot fiery glances in all directions.

'Most men would think it an honour to be chosen to play at all,' Will said civilly, and drove his elbow into Giles's midriff. The arm slackened, Giles exhaled mightily and fell over backwards, kicking out as he went and landing a glancing blow on the back of Will's thigh. Will, expecting it to engage higher up, leaped sideways and tripped over Giles. They closed and rolled in the dirt while Henry skipped aside and stood well back out of the way of feet and fists. Several people stopped to watch. Robert Croft, coming down the street with his son, took in the situation at a glance.

'Isn't that our dramatist?' Robert said. 'Who is he trying to strangle?'

'Giles Butcher,' Adrian said. 'There's a lot of ill-feeling among some of the boys who are to play women.'

'Giles Butcher's playing a woman?' Robert said, wonderingly. 'Can't you do better than that?' He delivered a judicious kick. 'That's enough, lads. Break it up before someone calls a constable.'

They got to their feet, Robert assisting Giles with a firm grasp of his collar. Adrian seized Will and hung on.

'I'll not be in his whoreson play,' Giles snarled. 'I'll break his neck first.'

'And I after him,' Henry said, seeing that it was now safe to join in.

'Now, Giles, I'm ashamed of you,' Robert said. 'To see my own Godson brawling in the street. Would you spoil this play when everyone is working so hard on it?'

'I'll spoil his face for him.'

'No, you won't. Your father's on the council with me. What will he say when I tell him? And you, Henry, for shame. What parts do you play?'

'He's a gentlewoman,' Henry said, pointing north-west of Giles who was bleeding at the nose and lip, eyelid purple and pulpy. 'I'm the Duchess of Hungary. I have to bear a son!'

'On stage?' Robert said. 'You amaze me. Not even Lord Leicester's Men could bring that off convincingly.'

'No, not on stage. But I have to stand there and say to the Duke — that's him, the bastard . . .' he glared at

Will '. . . I have to say, "Dear heart, thou knowst I am with child." '

Will had come out of the battle with nothing more than a bruise below his eye. Giles had seriously underestimated his adversary.

'Why did you say you'd be in it if you were going to end up fighting like this? You knew Adrian chose you for your voices.'

'That was before we read the parts,' Giles said. 'It's not what we have to say, it's what gets said about us, all about our pretty ways and honeyed lips and − and . . .' his voice sank to a whisper '. . . our Parian marble breasts.'

'No one says that *you* have a Parian marble breast,' Will said, 'you great cheese.'

'No, that's Gilbert, and I hope he sticks your compasses up your nose. I have George Wainwright running after me and begging for a kiss. *And it's meant to be funny!*' Giles roared.

'By God it's not,' Robert said, straight-faced.

'We can't lose all our women,' Will said. 'Stephen Thacker tells me his brother's no better, his foot and leg being swelled up to the knee. And that *really* isn't funny,' he said to Giles. 'Didn't you know how ill he is? Stephen may be in no mood to play at all.'

'I hope you look on poor Philip's affliction as more than an inconvenience,' Robert said. 'See here, boys, this will not do. If you undertook to play then you must keep your word. Will, can you not cut out some of the . . . courtesies?'

'I'll write instead that he's a poxy trollop with a jaw like an anvil and paps like the pimples on an alewife's arse,' Will said, 'if that will make him happy.'

He spent a chaste May Eve at Adrian's house, making diplomatic amendments as Robert Croft had suggested, and killing off the old Duchess to make way for a younger version.

'No Parian marble breasts,' Adrian reminded him. 'No honeyed lips nor teeth of Orient pearl. Giles can still slaughter you when the play is over and done.'

From outside they could hear tantalizing whoops and shrieks from the May revellers heading for the woods, but they bent over the work in hand, writing alterations to all the relevant parts, which had had to be collected in again, since Gilbert refused point blank to do it. Some players had been deeply reluctant to part with theirs, suspecting that they might not get them back.

'I know your plan,' Richard had said, 'you'll take it from me and give it to another that can read and I shall be left to cry "Aye" and "Shame" with Jakey.'

Someone tapped on the window in passing; Adrian looked up in time to see a grinning face and lewd gesticulations, but he also noticed, on the far side of the street, Katherine Page walking in close conference with that scurvy knave from the woollendraper's in Henley Street.

Perfidious jade, he thought, borrowing a line from the play where Honorius had been deceived into thinking that his wife had cuckolded him. Still, if Kate had transferred her inconstant affections to the woollendraper's journeyman, he could at least direct Stephen Thacker with an open mind.

The streets were empty by the time they finished work.

'To the Bear?' Adrian suggested. 'We've earned it – no, leave the playbook here,' he said, as Will started to scramble the papers together. Let him take it away and he would start altering it again.

Turning into Meer Pool Lane they saw a small female figure hurrying towards them.

'A maiden in distress?' Will said. 'Is anyone chasing her?'

'Better she runs towards us than from us,' Adrian said. 'But isn't it your Joan?'

It was; knees and elbows pumping, apron flapping, she stumbled up the street, not recognizing who was in front of her. When she looked up, only a yard or two from collision, she saw two strangers in her way, squawked with impatience, and sidestepped. Will caught her arm.

'Joan, what's amiss? Has someone ill-used you?'

She jerked her arm free. 'No. Leave go, Will. It's Mammy, the baby. I'm going for the midwife.'

He managed to intercept her before she ran on. 'Has she women with her?'

Adrian noted with amusement and affection her little-girl's face uplifted with feminine scorn. This was women's business.

'Of course. *We* knew. So would have you, if you had eyes to see. Nothing's amiss.'

'Go home, Joan. I'll run for the midwife.'

'Oh!' She twitched away again with an exasperated snort. 'What do *you* know?' She was not going to be balked of her rights and duties. 'Go to the Bear, you'll be out of the way.'

Adrian pulled Will on as he seemed inclined to hover. 'Let her alone. Women must take care of these things as they see fit. They don't want men around.'

'She's not a woman.'

'Tonight she is. Don't spoil it for her.'

'I wonder if she's thrown Father and Gilbert out as well,' Will said. 'Someone should be there for poor Dick. I was only his age or thereabouts when Joan was born. I heard Mother crying out and was scared to death. I thought they were butchering her, but it was a quick delivery. She had a three-day labour with Dick . . . I don't remember Gilbert at all. But she's not young,' he said. 'We were all amazed when we found out that she was carrying again – she thought all that was over. But after we lost little Anne last year she said that perhaps the Lord had sent her one last lamb to comfort her old age.'

Coming down Henley Street they could hear the screams, prayers and blasphemies mixed. Agitated shadows flitted across upper windows, downstairs his father could be seen, pacing up and down, up and down in front of the cold hearth, hands clasped, head bowed.

'I think God must forgive women for what they say in childbirth,' Adrian said wanly.

'Go on down to the Bear,' Will said. 'I'll join you if all's well. I must see after Dick.'

Who might be motherless by morning, Adrian thought, but did not say. He was about to move on, reluctantly, when someone came along the side of the house from the garden.

'Have you seen Joan?'

'Gilbert? Why aren't you with Dick?'

'I can't get him out of the henhouse.'

'What's he doing in the henhouse?'

'Joan sent him to shut up the hens and he's crawled in with them.'

'A May Eve to remember,' Adrian remarked as they followed Gilbert into the twilit garden. Will went down on hands and knees and put his head in at the low door. He could see nothing but he heard the hens stirring and a subdued whimpering.

'Leave me be.'

'You come on out, Dick, or I'll come in after you and we'll all be stifled, you, me and the hens. You can't stay in there, Sir Solomon will think you mean to cuckold him.'

'I don't think he'll understand that,' Adrian said, and was faintly shocked to hear Dick's knowing giggle. But he was crying again when he crawled out, shedding straw and feathers.

They stood round him helplessly.

'Joan won't have time for him, shall we take him to the Bear?' Will said. Adrian was not enthusiastic. Left in the charge of his brothers he had too often found himself kicking his heels in the Hart Royal while they caroused with friends. It had been interesting, but not much fun. Poor Dick; God keep his mammy safe.

'He can sit with Gerald's wife, perhaps. She's raising six, she'll understand.' They trailed down to the inn. The Bear was almost empty, most of the usual customers being out in the woods to bring home the May, and Adam was, they supposed, with David. He would never leave his old friend to go a-Maying.

Gerald's wife swept up Dick and bore him away to her kitchen. 'He can stay here for the night,' she said. 'I'll put him in with the others, poor babe, but if he curls up with the dogs I'll not disturb him. They're like puppies at that age anyway.'

They took a drink, more for companionship's sake than pleasure, lingering unhappily over it. Gilbert sprawled on the bench, elbows on table, and tried to seem manly, prefacing every remark with oaths that would have made a shipman flinch. What they all wanted was to be very small again, with a lap to climb into, and thought enviously of Dick in the kitchen, pillowed on the cushiony bosom of the innkeeper's wife.

Henley Street was hushed when they walked unwillingly home again. There was no sound but the voice of the bellman telling the hour in Meer Pool Lane. The house was eerily still.

'Is all well, do you think?'

'I hear no weeping. They'd have sent to find us if aught had gone amiss.' Will laid his hand to the latch. Before he could lift it the door was swept open from inside, and on the threshold stood Joan, holding up a candle but luminous herself with joy and self-importance, to tell them that their mother lived, and they had a new brother.

On Sunday John Shakespeare came to church for the first time in a long while, and after matins he stood at the font with Will, Gilbert and Dick. Joan carried the baby who was baptized Edmund, after his uncle, down from Wilmcote for the occasion, standing as Godfather.

He had ridden over alone, to Joan's disappointment; she was named for her aunt, but if Aunt Joan had been there she would not now be standing at the font herself to receive Edmund back from the Parson. She tried to look solemn and pious, but when she turned to face them all she was beaming helplessly. Will felt he could safely assume that he was at last forgiven for his part in the slaying of Dorcas.

Edmund was screaming passionately. A good sign, people said, approvingly. Had he remained docile, Will guessed, they would have said the same thing. It was only kind, whatever they might think privately, but Edmund so far was a promising baby, healthy and pink, with signs of the family hair, dark and frizzled. If Mother were willing – and he had better not mention it until her lying-in was over – they might perhaps borrow him for the final moments of the play. It was easy enough to produce a swaddled cushion for an infant on stage, he had seen it done, but when Giles Butcher, as the gentlewoman, came on to announce, with a final flourish:

'My lord, prepare to arm yourself with joy.
The Duchess is delivered of a boy,'

how much more realistic if he carried Edmund in his arms. Edmund could be let out of swaddling for the occasion, he might even wave a tiny fist. Then, when the Duke proclaimed:

'Put off all grief, this doleful night is run.
Salute the morn of our new-risen sun,'

he could hold up the baby, his new-risen son. It was a good play on words; Will was rather pleased with that. Then for the dance – which reminded him that he must do something about the music.

Every time he heard the turgid moans of Jakey's bagpipe he made a note to do something about the music. If Jakey were set on playing he could furnish something in the nature of a dirge, off-stage, when the Duke learned of Francisco's death.

Philip did not attend the next rehearsal, but Stephen reported that poultices seemed to be bringing down the swelling, although his fever did not break. Giles doubled for him with unseemly eagerness, having been offered Fabio as a sop to his wounded pride. He was hoping, no doubt, that Philip would be indisposed for so long that the part would become his by default. Stephen relinquished it with bad grace and went back to being a wife.

' "How now, friend Valentine," ' Giles trilled, ' "tell me how things stand, Between the Duke and his two noble sons." '

Anthony told him at length, explaining how the identical twin infants had grown to be strikingly dissimilar men. The necessity for this speech became apparent when Hugh and Adam entered with their wives. Hugh *must* have a beard, Adrian decided. Twins? They did not even look like brothers.

' "I must awhile attend his noble Grace," ' Anthony declaimed; ' "But lately come from his new marriage bed." '

'What new marriage bed?' Giles demanded. 'I thought this old Duchess was mother to grown men.'

'My fault.' Will riffled frantically through the playbook. 'I forgot to copy the lines where Valentine explains that the old Duchess died and the Duke has taken a new young wife. Don't worry about it now, leave your part at the end – and yours, Giles. Gilbert can copy it in.'

'I'll hell as like. You do it.'

'But I've *learned* it,' Anthony said, aggrieved.

'Then you'll have to unlearn it. The play makes no sense unless we know the Duchess is not the mother of these men. We've been through all this. How can Henry play mother to Adam?'

'You're playing his father.'

'I shall have a beard. The Duchess has no beard.'

'I don't *need* to have a baby,' Henry ventured rashly. Will and Adrian rounded on him.

'Yes you do!'

'This is a Whitsun pastime,' Adrian said. 'It has to end happily.'

'I thought it was a tragical history,' Henry said.

'It's a load of old rubbish,' someone said, keeping his head down.

'Oh, well, if that's what you think of it—' Will cried, making as if to rip the playbook in half.

'No!' Adrian snatched it away. 'It's enough of a rat's nest as it is. I wish you'd let it alone. *I'm* the bookholder. God's teeth, will you all get back to your places? Fabio and Valentine – *Valentine* – that's you, Anthony; stand back where you were. Duke – Will – come in with the Duchess. "Good Valentine, good Fabio, welcome both . . ." '

Will spoke his lines in toneless lumps as though he had no idea of what they meant. Considering who wrote them . . . Adrian thought, but let him get on with it. Likely his mind was elsewhere, trying to mend the holes in the plot which had begun to show only when they put on their parts, like worn hose. There were no more interruptions until the Duke, having announced his plan to let his sons rule half the country each, turned to his Duchess:

> 'Madam, behold you where the moon's great
>   orb
> Like a pale mirror to the sun's fair face
> Hangs in the west—'

'Hold hard,' Wat called out. 'What hour of the clock is it?'

'Past seven,' Will said.

'Not now, in the play.'

'It's evening in the play, too.'

'Then what's the full moon doing in the west? It rises at sunset, in the east.'

'I mis-wrote it. I meant east.'

'How if there is no full moon that night?' Richard said.

Things ground to a halt again. The company gathered round. 'There was a full moon the last two nights. There'll be no full moon at Whitsun, it's only three weeks to go.'

'Mayhap it will be overcast,' Matt said.

'How if it rains?'

'We'll play rain or shine. Rain never stopped Essex's Men, did it?'

'Nay, but if it rains, there'll be no moon.'

'There'll be no kind of a moon at all,' Will said. 'We'll be playing in broad daylight. We don't need a moon.'

'But you said, the Duke said, "Behold the moon's fat face—" '

'Perhaps one can stand with a counterfeit moon hanging on a string from a pole,' Hugh suggested.

'No!' Will howled. 'If I say "Behold the moon," the audience will know that there's a moon up there to behold.'

'Why should they believe you?' Giles asked.

'For the same reason they'll believe I'm a Duke and you're a gentlewoman. It's a *play*. When you see a play you believe what you hear.'

'When I see a play, the players know what they're doing.'

'So shall we know what we are doing,' Adrian said. 'We'll do what *I* say. Go back to Will's speech, "Madam behold you where the moon's great orb . . ." '

'Hangs in the *east*,' Wat said.

There followed a touching scene in which the young Duchess confided to her husband that in a seven-month she should bear him a child:

'As doth the moon wax great then so shall I,
For as it is with women, 'tis with me.
There beats a second heart within this breast.'

'Do people really talk to each other like that?' Richard wondered. 'When my old lady told me our Thomas was on the way she just said, "Dick, I've fallen again".'

'They are the nobility,' Wat said. 'They don't talk like us.'

'No doubt they swive like us, though,' Richard said. 'Same result.'

'Where's the gentlewoman?' Adrian said. 'The Duchess has called for her gentlewoman.'

'I'm Fabio now,' Giles said, complacently, from a safe distance.

'Fabio does not appear again in this scene,' Adrian said. 'When you are not Fabio you are the gentlewoman.'

'I can't be both at once.'

'You are each by turns,' Adrian said, 'and when Philip is well you will be the gentlewoman only.'

Giles stamped forward, glowering.' "What is my lady's pleasure?" '

'Say it like a woman,' Adrian pleaded. 'You curtsey when you speak.'

'How do I curtsey?'

'You've seen it done.'

'Yes, but not *how*. I don't know where women put their feet when they do it. It's all hidden in their skirts.'

'You've got three sisters, ask them,' Henry said. 'Just give at the knees for now.'

It was beginning to get dark. Adrian was anxious to try the conversation between the brothers when they pledged to support each other through their father's absence. Fabio turned up after that and revealed to Francisco the Duke's true purpose in dividing the country, setting the tragedy in motion. It was a crucial moment. He wanted to see, more particularly wanted the others to see, Adam in action, how a real player could hold the stage.

Having got the brothers face to face he was struck by a troubling thought. The same idea had evidently occurred to Richard who was counting on his fingers. As Francisco responded to Honorius's declaration of brotherly love with a similar avowal, Richard leaped up.

'How long before these men kill each other?'

'They don't kill each other, the first kills the second.' Wat had appointed himself official interpreter, and in truth he seemed to have grasped the story faster than anyone else. 'This will all unfold as the weeks pass.'

'It'll be a mighty short pregnancy, then,' Richard said, 'if she's but two months gone and the babe's to be born at the end of the play.'

'It could be born early,' Jakey said. 'With all these murders and ghosties the shock may bring her on – a seven-month babe.'

'They don't thrive though,' Matt said. 'Not at seven months.'

'I don't think this matters,' Adam said. As usual, all argument ceased as soon as he spoke. 'All we need is for Will to write in a line or two – Now seven-nights nine have passed – or some such.'

Richard, the mathematician, was at it again. 'Sixty-three days? 'Why sixty-three days?'

'Or some such, I said.' Adam was showing signs of irritation, rare for him. Adrian thought of those precarious humours. 'It could be seven-nights twelve or fortnights four. It's only to show that time has passed.'

'Will Henry have to wear a great belly under his skirt?' Stephen said, lasciviously. 'One that waxes greater as time passes?'

'That I'll not,' Henry snapped. 'I'm not seen again until after the babe is born.'

'Yes you are, outside Francisco's gate, after the murder. Look at your part for God's sake,' Will said. 'After the babe is born you're not seen at all.'

'Perhaps you die in childbed?' Giles suggested.

'Nay, it has a happy ending,' Wat said. 'Now, shut up, all of you! Adam was in the middle of his speech.'

'Why are you in such a hurry?' George demanded.

'When these noblemen are done talking of noble things, why then it's our turn,' Wat said. 'Haven't you studied your part neither, George Wainwright, and you able to read? When the brothers go out – *exeunt* – then on comes Barnard and Tobias their servants, that's you and Richard, and I, Ralph the clown, and we have some excellent fooling.'

'We'll be here till Doomsday before we get any kind of fooling at this rate,' Matt said. 'And speaking for myself, I can fool as easily at the Bear or the Hart Royal as I can here in the churchyard.'

'I don't think we'll get to your scene tonight,' Adrian said. 'The light will be gone soon and we can't play in the dark.'

'Then why are we here?' George said. 'Why must we listen to all these others and never speak ourselves?'

'So that you get to know the whole play and not just your parts in it,' Will said. 'Maybe then you'll all stop asking damnfool questions.'

He had repossessed the playbook and was making further adjustments concerning, Adrian hoped, the length of the Duchess's pregnancy.

Nine

David died in the night. No passing bell rang but the
news spread quickly through the company who turned
out on the morrow evening to follow him to church for
the last time. Gerald, the host of the Bear, paid for the
bell and pall for the old man's final journey. They stood
at the graveside to bid him farewell, Jakey at a respectful
distance, ready to spring into action as soon as the
mourners had gone.

Will and Adrian had arranged a rehearsal for that
evening but it was delayed by a day out of respect for the
dead harper.

'Did he die in his sleep?' Will asked Adam.

'In a happy state, I think; he did not know whether he
woke or slept, but he was at peace.'

'Even without a priest?' Adrian said.

'Aye, he had a priest.' Adam spoke quietly. 'He died
shriven.'

'How? Where?'

'It was after midnight,' Adam said, 'the moon behind
the clouds. He was uneasy at first, hearing owls, begging

that we should soon be on our way so as to reach the holy brothers in time. So I told him, "Have you forgotten, Davy? We reached the brothers yesternight. This is the Hospital of Saint John Baptist in Warwick." So he asked me to fetch one of the brothers to him, and so I went out . . .'

'And when you came back he had died? What could you have done otherwise, fetched the Parson?' Will said.

'I found a priest,' Adam said. 'I came back with a little sweet oil that I had by me from the apothecary, and a little wafer of bread that may be got anywhere. Then in the darkness I sat by him, hooded, in the person of a priest, and heard his confession. Then I anointed him and gave him the viaticum and held the crucifix before his eyes. The moon came out just in time. His eyes were dim. He saw the cross, not how I had bound two laths together, nor that there was no dying Christ upon it.

'And then I saw that it was time, so I opened the window and he knew that his soul might depart in peace through it. And out it went, into the moonlight.'

'You played the priest, Adam?' Adrian said. He felt that he ought to be shocked, but he was not.

'To let a good old man die in his own faith. Yes. I did ill in the sight of God according to the Church, perhaps I have committed a hanging offence, or a burning offence, but who was harmed by it? David thought he was off to purgatory but he knew his friends would pray for his soul and speed it soon to heaven. Well, now we are told there is no purgatory, and we living can do nothing for the grateful dead. Is Davy standing before the Judgement Seat now, as we speak? Or does his soul sleep until the last trumpet is blown on Doomsday? Or is there, as I sometimes think, no heaven nor hell neither, no Doomsday, no last trump, and does Davy sleep his last sleep in the grave for eternity? Don't mind me, boys, I'm no heretic. I'm mad, remember?'

'Where are you going now?' Will said.

'To get drunk.'

They watched him leave the churchyard, stately, a little drunk already. Behind them a shovel bit into loose earth. Jakey was getting to work.

'If he tells others in his cups what he told us he could be in most fearsome trouble,' Adrian said. 'Thank God Hugh was not here to hear him.'

'Where is Hugh?'

'Gone over to Charlcote on some errand, fleeces or wool.'

'He'd have missed the rehearsal,' Will said.

'Then you must give thanks that Davy's funeral prevented it,' Adrian said tartly. 'Surely it was Divine Intervention that sent Hugh away this evening. A jealous God would have made certain that Hugh heard what Adam said. I think we should keep Adam company this evening.'

'I'll be with you shortly,' Will said. 'I want to speak with Jakey, first.'

'About the music? I'm off before he starts playing that lament he promised. Whenever I hear the bagpipe I want to piss.'

Will returned to the graveside.

'Stand clear of my elbow,' Jakey said. He had established a rhythm pivoting on his own axis, thrusting the shovel into the hillock of earth, up, round, overturning it into the pit and swinging back again before the bladeful landed on the shrouded corpse, already half concealed.

'Hard work, Jakey?'

'This part's easy. 'tis the digging that puts a knife in a man's back.'

'Soil too heavy?'

'Not this spring. Plaguey dry.'

'But not in winter, surely?'

'Plaguey wet. But 'tisn't winter, is it? Our Davy will lie dry till Swithunmas at least, God willing.'

'What of the worms?'

'Earthworms?'

'Graveworms.'

'Funny you should ask that,' Jakey said, never interrupting his steady swing. 'One time we dug a grave, for a weaver it was, and got the wrong place. I doubt I should be telling you this, Will, but you won't peach on old Jakey, will you? We were ill-informed and down we went, and it seemed to me then, although I was new to the work, that the earth was coming up very easy. Still, as I said, I was new to the work, it wasn't my place to ask what was going on. Well, I'd seen skulls and bones come up before, as they do, but then my spade hits something soft, softer than the earth. I was down in the hole but I can tell you, I was up out of it like there was a fiend biting my ballocks. Damage was done though. It was no bones I'd hit, it was a corpse, still in its winding sheet though there wasn't much of that left. It was an ill sight, I can tell you, not meant by God for man to see, but I never saw hide nor hair of a worm. Earthworms, yes, wiggling their pointy heads through the spade cuts, but not worms in the corpse.

'I don't know. Everyone says that the worms devour us, and when I was new to the work I used to have foul dreams about it, when I saw visitings of people I'd helped bury come back in the dark, with all their horrid graveclothes hanging off their yellow bones and the worms gnawing away at their vitals, but all these years since, I've never seen a worm.'

Will had given Honorius some stirring lines on the subject, after Francisco's murder:

> For now does sharp remorse devour my heart
> As do the worms devour my brother's corse.

And hath the worm's sharp tooth bit keener in
Than my sore conscience enbiteth me?

He had wanted to check with Jakey that graveworms really did have teeth. Jakey, he had been confident, would be in a position to know, and yet here he was, doubting that they existed at all. Well, no, he had not quite said that, Will argued with himself, only that he personally had never seen one.

Unless Jakey was, like Wat only more courteously, telling him to mind his own trade.

Jakey continued his swing, the crunch of the shovel in earth at one end of it, the heavy dump of falling clods at the other.

'When I've done,' Jakey said, 'I'll play him a solemn tune to help him on his way. I've brought my pipe. You'll remember me and my pipe in the play, won't you, Will? Let it be set down that I am to be paid fourpence for playing the pipe, same as for digging a grave. I'll give you a most heavy sad dirge for that dead brother of yours, Francisco, and my "Aye" and "Shame" with the best of them.'

In the glove shop next morning Stephen reported on Philip's progress in graphic detail.

'Well, I told you how fast his foot did swell, first red, then purple like a plum, then there was streaks of green and the swelling came up over his ankle and crept towards his knee, and that split and wept with a terrible stink,' Stephen said. 'And out of that came like a fiery finger, along his thigh. We thought that when the poison reached his heart, he'd die, but then old Mother Margaret from Swine Street came with her poultices and words.'

'What words?' Will said. 'These words she said over the wound – prayers?'

'If they were prayers,' Stephen said, 'they weren't any I ever heard Parson speak. It was all mumble mumble mumble arbli-garblus.'

'Latin?'

'I know Latin,' Stephen snapped. 'As well as you do. It wasn't Latin. I asked Philip after but he was in such a fever he might have taken English for Greek.'

'Witchcraft?' Martin suggested.

'If it was witchcraft it wrought a good thing,' Will said. 'Philip's fever is down. A week ago he was like to die, now he's well and like to live. It seems to me only God could have a hand it that. Don't let's talk of witchcraft and get a good old woman into trouble.'

'But she might have been praying to Satan,' Martin said.

'Why should she ask the devil to do a good deed? Aren't such things in God's hand? If God had meant Philip to die he would have died, don't you think?'

'Now he's better you'll be stuck with him for Fabio,' Gilbert said.

'I don't know about that,' Stephen said. 'He can't put foot to ground and he's hardly any voice left, high or low.'

'Better let Giles go on playing Fabio, then,' Gilbert said. 'He's as miserable as sin since everyone found out he was a gentlewoman.'

'But he doesn't sound like a man.'

'I'll tell him that.' Gilbert whipped round the cutting bench, out of arm's length. 'Must go, I'll be late for school. I'll tell you what, though. If you can't find anyone else to join the company and have to make one of us double, there's someone who's never on at the same time as the gentlewoman.'

'Who does he mean?' Will said. Gilbert was already out of the house.

'You should know,' Stephen said. 'Think about it.'

'Adrian's got the playbook.' Adrian was clinging to it fiercely on the grounds, he said, that he needed to study it the better to know what was happening on stage without having to look. Will suspected that Adrian was afraid that if he got his hands on it again he would make more alterations.

And he would. Every time he heard his words spoken he saw ways to amend them and all the time there were the most unlikely people noticing problems and discrepancies in the plot – Richard for instance. The workmen were all the same, unable to imagine anything, unable to conceive of anyone else imagining anything. But he could not fault them for that. Their livelihoods depended on them knowing the facts, being accurate, their very lives, even. Look at what one moment's inattention had cost Matt. He might have broken his neck in that fall from the tithe-barn roof; even so, he would never hold his head up straight again.

Bless Richard Fisher, who knew the phases of the moon so well but still thought that they must have a moon on stage. And damn Hugh who had to suggest that they hang up a plate on a string. Surely he should have known that someone had only to say, 'Well-met by moonlight', and there would *be* moonlight. The sooner Hugh put aside childish things and went off to Oxford for a physician the better, taking his prudish puritanism with him. Medicine was welcome to him. God forbid he should enter the Church and inflict his personal prejudices on everyone else. Now he was refusing to play the ghost, his own ghost as it were, on the grounds that damned souls could not return to earth and those in heaven would not want to. Therefore, it followed, any apparition claiming to be a dead man must be a deception of the devil.

Still, Will thought, if it hadn't been for Hugh worrying at the idea that it might be blasphemy to invent extra characters for the story of Abel's murder, he might never have wandered off into the exciting environs of Hungary, would not have discovered the Duke and his family. He would have been stuck with two brothers and God who might be omnipotent, omniscient, all-seeing, but as a character was hopelessly predictable.

He paused in his stitching to see if he were to be struck down palsied or dead for this awful thought but God, as he often suspected, had other things on His mind than Will Shakespeare's errant musings. Either He was counting falling sparrows as the Scriptures insisted, or He was steering the planets in their courses. He left it to men to burn, flay, dismember each other in His name, and there were men in Stratford, he knew, who might, having nothing better to do, take it upon themselves to hound harmless old Margaret Hope for a witch, because she knew more than they did. Philip could have lost his leg or his life without her intervention. Adrian had spoken of Philip dying of shame if they took the part of Fabio from him. How easy it was to speak of death; how easily death came among them.

At mid-morning a youth was shown into the shop. He stood in a shaft of sunlight, golden, immaculate, his hair and little beard sparkling with red lights. His hose were unwrinkled, his doublet fitted like a second skin under his short green velvet cloak. He had the colouring for green and knew it. Will had never seen so many shades of green in one outfit, down to his belt and the purse hanging from it, which he recognized as being of their own manufacture. So, this lad might look as though he had stepped down from gilded London among muddy yokels, but he bought his trappings from John Shakespeare at the High Cross on Market Day.

'I have come for the gloves,' he said.

'That is, on the whole, why people come here,' Will said. 'Which gloves had you ordered?'

'Not I,' the young man said. 'My master, Peter Starling.'

Behind him Stephen prowled a step or two on his toes and flapped suggestively with his elbows.

'Ah, the wedding order,' Will said. 'I'll fetch my father.'

The youth stepped in front of him. 'No excuses, boy. The gloves were promised for today. One-and-ninety pairs in leather and—'

'And the chicken-skins in a walnut.' Will measured him by eye. All his manhood was in the little dagger he wore at his belt, there was not much muscle under that doublet. He was several inches taller than Will and many pounds lighter. His centre of gravity was high. He would go over easily if Will put his head down . . . *Boy* . . .

Bastard.

'Well, normally we don't keep anything so curious lying about in the shop,' he said, gritting his teeth. 'If they were promised for today, then today they will be ready. We didn't gain our reputation by disappointing our customers.'

'Which reputation would that be?'

'The reputation,' Will said, holding his right fist down with his left, behind his back, 'that led your master to order his gloves from us and not from Quiney's, down the street. Stand aside, if you please. By what name shall I announce you?' *Swinesnout.*

The young man blushed. 'Master Capon.'

Stephen's chicken impersonation reached new heights. What a pity he was not in on the excellent fooling with Wat and his gang.

'Capon,' Will said deliberately. He went to the door and found his father crossing the passage to the hall, close enough for him not to have to raise his voice overmuch when he said, 'Father, here's one Master Capon, come for his chicken-skin gloves.'

Even John Shakespeare had trouble keeping a straight face. 'I'll fetch them,' was all he said.

It was no laughing matter. Perhaps chickens had thinner skins in London, or walnuts were larger. They had had to resort to a subterfuge. With luck, no one would notice.

Father came back carrying a little box which he laid on the bench before young Capon. They gathered round, Stephen now serious, as it was opened. Inside, on a pad of blue velvet, sat the walnut. It had been gilded, a tiny hinge set in the shell so that it opened like an oyster.

'Show me the tree where such walnuts grow!'

'Spanish, I believe,' Will said. They had contrived the cover story in advance.

'Ah, well, we are always on the lookout for such prodigies,' John said, 'knowing how popular they are for housing favours and notions.' He managed to imply that there was a constant demand for gilded walnuts. 'Please to open it, Master Capon, but pray do not take out the gloves. They have been cunningly rolled.'

'How can I tell if they be perfect?'

'Because they come from the workshop of John Shakespeare.' He dared him to contradict it. 'The one-and-ninety leather pairs are packed and ready. Do you want to try them all on?'

Capon was still marvelling at the walnut, as well he might. In despair they had resorted to Martin's brother for secret assistance. The walnut was carved from the wood of that same tree, to specification. A goldsmith had gilded it. The workmanship was masterly. If Capon, or Peter Starling himself, or the future Mistress Starling, were to be foolish enough to pick off the gilding they would discover what lay beneath, but no one looking at it would ever guess that this was the work of men, not God's own hand. The cost of it had cut into the profit from the gloves but John had overcharged for the capons in any case. Dorcas had not perished in vain.

Francisco lay dead. Honorius had not meant to slay him but at the height of their quarrel he had swung his staff dangerously close to his brother who had drawn his dagger. Honorius, warding off the blow, had struck him on the head and Francisco, mortally wounded, fell flat.

A heated argument broke out, largely as a result of the outburst of laughter that followed Francisco's mode of dying. Hugh sat up, scowling.

'What's so funny? Is a man's death an occasion for mirth, now?'

'It's the way you do it,' Wat said. 'Look, lad, when a man has his skull cracked open he doesn't go over backwards.'

'Why not? Where else will he go, upwards?'

'If he'd punched you on the jaw,' Richard explained, 'you'd have gone flying right enough, but he gets you smack on the pate.'

'He's right,' Adam said. Deferential silence fell, as usual. 'You'd go down on your knees, sway . . .' he went through the motions himself '. . . then fall forwards. You still have lines to say. "Go tell my widow I am foully slain. Francisco is a dead man, world adieu. I stay no more to look on life, and you." '

'On who?' Matt said.

'The world,' Adam told him swiftly, before anyone else could come up with an alternative theory. 'It will seem much more grievous if you speak them on your knees, dying, than if you fall down dead and have to sit up again.'

'Actually,' Adrian said, annoyed that Adam had come out with what he had been about to say himself, 'from where I'm standing, which is where the audience will be, it doesn't look as though he'd been slain at all. He seemed to stumble and fall over. Adam's staff never went anywhere near his head.'

'True,' George Wainwright chimed in from behind him. 'That staff went whistling past. Mind you, he's such a streak of piss a frog's fart would knock him down.'

Adam felt that his technique was under attack. 'This is the first time we've done it; Hugh must learn not to duck. There are ways of making a blow seem to fall. Hugh and I will practise on our own. You swing the staff thus, but just before it hits its target you must clench your hand and the swing is halted – *so*.' He demonstrated with panache; unfortunately Hugh chose that moment to stand up and the staff caught him across the neck.

'That's more like it!' George crowed. 'That looked like the real thing.'

'What are you doing back there?' Adrian turned on him. 'You're supposed to come on *now* and discover your master bending over his brother's corpse.'

The corpse was staggering to its feet, clutching its neck.

'No! Stay down, now,' Adrian called heartlessly. 'We'll run straight on.'

'With me half dead?'

'It's more lifelike than it was before. Sink to your knees, say your words and *die*, for God's sake. George! Get ready to go on when he's done dying – no, not now. Let him finish.'

Hugh croaked out his last words and collapsed, George hopping from foot to foot with impatience, while Adam, a murderer by mischance, stood aghast, clutching heart with one hand, brow with the other.

George pranced on. ' "I stay no more to look at life and you. Enter Tobias. Did you not call me, Master? Lord what's this that lies in horrid welter—" '

'No! You *don't* say "I stay no more to look on life and you", that's your cue. You *don't* say "Enter Tobias". That's what you *do*.'

'But it's all writ down here,' George said, waving his paper.

'That's so you know who speaks before you come on,' Wat called. 'Remember at the beginning when we all come on together?'

'Aye, but we *were* all together. I didn't have to remember that. Adam here said, "Come on, George," and on I came.'

'Well, you're on, now,' Adrian said. 'Just say your lines – no, don't go off again. Stay where you are.'

George stood like a scarecrow dangling from a post in a field of rye.

' "Did you not call me, Master?" ' He raised one arm, stiffly, and pointed. ' "Lord what's that that lies in horrid welter starkly there with both eye ope and fixed at thy feet my brother had a seizure and fell dead he's bleeding at the ears 'tis often thus." '

'How do we make him seem to bleed?' Richard asked.

'Go away, you're not in this scene,' Will said. 'Look, he's still saying his part cues and all. Adam never gets a word in.'

'They use pig's blood, so I've heard,' Wat said.

'What, kill a pig in May just for counterfeit blood?' Richard was scandalized. 'Maybe in London . . .'

'We'll get some pigment from the dyer's,' Will said. 'Look, Adam's right. Let them rehearse together, all three; the quarrel, the murder and Tobias discovering his master with the corpse. They drag it by the heels—'

'By the heels!' The corpse rose up again. 'I'll not be dragged by the heels.'

'Well, by the hair then, if you prefer,' Adrian snapped. 'Or by the ears. It's all one to me. You're dead. Tobias buries you privily but we don't see that. We'll go on to the next scene. Next scene! Duke, Duchess, Fabio, Valentine, gentlewoman, on: at the gate of Francisco's house. Then enter Francisco's wife.'

Was anyone going to believe that Will was Adam's father, even disguised in sheep's wool? – which reminded him, they had better set about procuring properties and costumes. In a real company these would be the most valuable things they owned. Here it would be a matter of begging and borrowing, though what woman would be happy to lend her finery to be tramped about in by three schoolboys and an apprentice? Apart from Mistress Pickering at the Hart Royal, whose girth was legendary, was there a woman in town whose clothes would fit Giles or Henry without splitting? He would have to canvass mothers and sisters to get busy with their needles.

Now that he knew his lines Will spoke them with more conviction, also eager, perhaps, to prove to Adam that in him, at least, was one who knew what he was doing. Henry held his hand reluctantly by the fingertips while Giles, determinedly flat-footed, plodded behind.

> 'How soft the setting sun, like to a nurse,
> Bestows her rosy mantle o'er these walls
> As on a cradle where the suckling babe
> Nests for the night.'

>   'Indeed a tender sight.
> But thought you not, my lord, to see your son
> Ride forth to greet us ere we reached this place?'

> 'My good Francisco finds the cares of state

Distract him sore, but here comes one in haste,' Will said. Nothing happened. '*HERE COMES ONE IN HASTE!*'

Stephen galloped on stage as if pursuing a runaway cow, but before he could get a word out a demonic howl drifted across the churchyard. Everyone stopped dead, gazing about; one or two furtively crossed themselves. Twilight was thickening, the mist was creeping up from the river in serpentine tentacles, like the wraiths of vipers.

The wail rose again, as from a dying lung full of phlegm. From behind a buttress a pale figure drifted towards them, moaning hideously.

'Jakey!

The gravedigger stopped and the moan subsided to a grunt. Adrian bore down on him.

'Jakey, what the devil are you doing?'

'Is it not now I play my hearty sad dirge? I saw the man kill his brother – *twice*,' he added.

'No, it is not now,' Adrian said.

'But he's dead. I spoke to Will at Davy's graveside. He's to put in a heavy dirge for me, he said.'

'Oh, did he? Well, wherever he's put it it won't be here.' He seized the bagpipe by the throat to jerk it from Jakey's embrace. Jakey clung on. Deflating, it exhaled a ghastly death rattle. 'Jakey, get this whoreson bladder out of here. If I hear it again, I'll shoot it, I'll strangle it, I'll kick it to Jericho and you after it.'

Wat intervened. 'That man's death is a murder, remember, to be kept secret. How can it be a secret if you come on whooping and hawking? I'll wager Will's written you a fine solemn part later on, when the death is discovered.'

'Do they dig him up, then?' Matt asked. 'We shall be playing on boards, shan't we? How can we dig a hole in oak planks?'

Jakey panicked. 'Nay, I can't say words but "Aye" and "Shame". I'll play my pipe. I can't speak.'

'You don't have any words,' Adrian said. 'Your part is all wheezing.

'No need to speak ill of my pipe, Master,' Jakey said, cradling it like a baby. 'It takes time to warm her up.'

'No one's speaking ill of your bagpipe, Jakey,' Will said, inaccurately, 'but you are not to lay a finger on it until we tell you to. And we shan't be getting to your part tonight.'

'What about my part?' Stephen demanded. 'Are we going to do this scene or not?'

'What's the use of trying?' Adrian said. 'It's almost too dark to see, and every man here must be up in the morning for work or school. Listen, all rehearsals are going to end like this, unfinished, scarce begun, unless we go straight through, no stumbling, no stopping, no

arguments about who does this or what means that –
straight through. When each scene is done I'll tell you
what I think and you can ask questions. Some of you
don't know your parts yet. Some of you know too much
of everyone's part but your own. Yes, I mean you, George.'

Ten

'Costumes and properties,' Robert Croft said. 'Well, of course you must have them, but surely they come out of the nine and sevenpence?'

'Of course they do,' Adrian said. 'We're not asking for more money, we just don't know how to set about it. Properties are easy – swords, staves, jugs, flagons, they can all be contrived or borrowed. Giles and Will have got their sisters making beards, for those who cannot grow their own. And costumes – well, we need cloaks and robes and hats and ruffs, but such we can fashion out of our own things with some laces and fur to dress them up. It's the women that's the trouble.'

'It always is,' Robert said. 'Ah, and such women; maidens to stir a man's hot blood.'

'No, sorry, Father, three wives, one of them a Duchess great with child, and a gentlewoman who looks as if she could throw an ox over a stile.'

'You aren't seriously keeping young Butcher on as a gentlewoman?' Robert said.

'He's hoping we'll keep him on as Fabio,' Adrian said, 'and we would, if only he didn't pipe like a titlark.'

'Does that matter so very much? After all, doesn't Anthony play Valentine?'

'Yes, but his voice is low. He can pass for a man of middle years.'

'In the dark with the light behind him. You'll never borrow a gown to fit across Giles's shoulders,' Robert said. 'If only your mother were still alive, she could whip up a wedding gown out of a sheet.'

'Talking of sheets,' Adrian said, 'we have to dress a ghost.'

'Why do you need a sheet?'

'That's what Will's written in the playbook: *Enter the Ghost in his winding sheet.*'

'But isn't it the ghost of Francisco, foully slain and privily buried in a ditch? Don't tell me his guilty brother stops to wrap him in a shroud.'

'Well, it all happens off-stage since we can't dig a ditch, as Matt points out. No, the real problem is, Hugh is playing Francisco but he won't play the Ghost because he says it is contrary to Holy Writ that a man's spirit should walk the earth. So we plan for the Ghost to be played by someone else, wearing the sheet. I don't know who. We are down to thirteen players now. Philip is ill and two of the others wearied of crying "Aye" and "Shame" and went home.'

'Wouldn't it be easier to have someone else playing Francisco *and* the Ghost: someone who doesn't have Hugh's scruples about causing offence in heaven?'

'It's a bit late for that. I'm surprised he still wants to be in it at all, but at first he thought it was going to be a plain story, Cain killing Abel, and he was quite happy to be Abel. The story grew under his feet once Will got to work on it. I think by the time we have finished he will be against all plays.'

'I don't know where he gets his puritan notions,' Robert said. 'Your uncle has never cared much for the good life. This winding sheet, I take it you'll have it sorely rent by many wounds and streaked with blood?'

'Something like that,' Adrian said. 'The more blood the better.'

'Then you'd better beg a sheet that's seen some wear. I'd suggest Mistress Pickering, she's not over-particular about the company she keeps and her sheets will have been very well-used. Do you know that old tale of the bawd and the knight who kept his spurs on – no? Never mind, I shouldn't be the one to tell it to you. Ask at the Bear, they're sure to have some, old and torn. What will you do for blood?'

'Real companies use pigs' blood, I'm told, but all we need for the murder is a little madder to smear in Hugh's ears after he's slain. I can drag the sheet around the shambles.'

'I'll see what I can do about your wives and Duchesses,' Robert said. 'As for the gentlewoman, I'd advise a smock with a bodice laced over it. You'll never get Giles into a gown. Anything else?'

'We need a pipe-and-tabor man for the dance at the end – and perhaps for a jig in the middle when Wat and the servants do their fooling. Wat has worked up some fine business with a ladder and a laundry basket. Will didn't like it at first because they wouldn't stay with what he'd written for them, but Wat soon put him right. It's much funnier now.'

'And Jakey's bagpipe will not suffice, even with Wat in full flow?'

'Don't!' Adrian clasped his ears. 'It sounds like swine being butchered. It sounds like souls in torment. It sounds like the rape of the Sabine women. I can just about stand it when he's actually playing, it's the warming-up that's not to be endured. He might as well stick a reed up a peacock's arse and blow, he'd get much the same noise. No, Jakey will do very well for the dirge, which we have only put in to make him happy, and perhaps for the Ghost. Perhaps not.'

'Doesn't it speak?'

'Only to cry "Honorius, dishonour'd Honorius".'

'How shall people know who it is, then? If Hugh is not to play it I suppose you won't be able to show its face.'

'Oh, Honorius speaks to it, no one else can see it, you see. "It is my brother's spirit sues me here" and "Spirit avaunt! I was thy brother ere I was thy murderer!" '

'So you need not show it at all.'

'That's a thought,' Adrian said. 'You mean, just have Honorius gibbering and pointing and seeming to speak to thin air as if he were run mad. It would be an effect – but I'm not sure that people would understand. I'm not sure that most of our players would understand. They have little faith in illusion. When Honorius cries "Look, where it comes again!" it ought to have been seen to go away so that the audience can see it coming back. Its very presence should unfix our hair – that's what Will says, anyway.'

Adam came to rehearsal with the sheet, courtesy of the Bear, already knotted at the top and artistically dabbled with blood about the head and shoulders.

'I know you meant it to be rent,' he explained, 'but after all, the death blow is a single clout with a staff. And since Hugh and I have rehearsed the quarrel and the murder it would be a pity to have to go back and contrive a different death with sword cuts. Though perhaps Hugh could fall upon his dagger as he goes down.'

'Will can write in a line for you about shrouding the

corpse,' Adrian said. 'He went at it so fast he never noticed where one part did not accord with another. After all, Honorius did not mean to slay Francisco, it was done in a moment of rage. He'd bury the corpse properly if he could.'

'Who is to play the Ghost?' Adam said. 'I take it Hugh still refuses.'

'Will was going to do it, but that won't work if he's playing the Duke. The Ghost appears three times to Honorius; once when he is before the Duke, his father, the second time when he is with his wife, about to go to bed, and the third time when he is alone; so *you* can not play it, Will can not play it, and Gilbert can not, being the wife.'

'We could all take turns under the sheet,' Adam said. 'No – that was a jest. Your players are already better at each other's parts than they are at their own.'

'It'd be a rare fine part to play.' Wat had come up behind them. 'I'll be your ghost, Adrian.' He put on a reedy voice. 'Here comes I, old dead Francisco's spirit.' He seized the sheet and draped it over his head. It hung some way short of his ankles.

'That's not what Will's written for it, has he?' Adam said, shocked.

'No, but when Wat's in the Mummers' play at Christmas, that's how he comes on: *Here comes I, Saint George, the valiant man.* No, Wat, you're too big to be

Francisco's ghost. Hugh's half your size. You stick to your fooling.'

'I never saw a ghost in a play,' Wat said. 'Might not the people be affrighted? We don't want women and green girls fainting at the sight of it.'

'On the whole, Wat, I doubt if it will be convincing enough for that,' Adam said. 'No offence, Adrian. Played on a winter's night, with candles, you might get away with it, but I think by day people will know it is a counterfeit spirit. Here's Stephen. What news of Philip?'

'Out of his fever,' Stephen said, 'and just beginning to hobble about, but he's in no fit state to play.'

'That settles it, then,' Adrian said. He hoisted himself on to the wall and cupped his hands around his mouth. 'Company, to me!'

They gathered below him like sheep at a gate, gazing earnestly.

'We are all met? Good. One who can't be here is Philip Thacker. He'll live, thank God, but he won't be playing, so some parts that have been changed must stay changed. Giles, you will play Fabio. Matt, you will take Giles's place as the gentlewoman.'

'I play a woman?' Matt looked incredulous, as well he might. Giles's smile split his face.

'You'll be well-wimpled, no one will know it is you.' He had a sudden horrible premonition of the squinting Duchess and her wry-necked gentlewoman in hapless collision. 'And you have not much to say, only a few lines.'

'But I know my words,' Matt protested. 'I cry "Aye" and "Shame" with Jakey.'

'We'll find someone else to cry "Aye" and "Shame",' Adrian said. 'Or maybe we'll do without. There's altogether too much "Aying" and "Shaming". Henry, you are to play the Ghost.'

'And not the Duchess?' Henry was transfigured with joy. His eye went every which way.

'*And* the Duchess,' Adrian said remorselessly. 'The Ghost and the Duchess never appear at the same time and you are a quick study. You can easily learn the Ghost's part.'

'Nay, let *me* play the Ghost,' Matt said. 'I can be a woman, but not gentle.'

'Let Hugh play the Duchess. All this is his fault—'

'That's enough!' Wat bellowed. 'You should be ashamed of yourselves. Here's Will writ a marvellous play for us all and Adrian's wearing himself to a shard making it all come about, and you lads witter and bicker about being ghosts and women. This is a play!' he roared. 'There's no shame in putting on a skirt. Henry, you're the Duchess. Matt, you are the Ghost.' He rose and swelled magnificently. '*I'll* play the gentlewoman.'

An awe-struck silence fell. Will caught Adrian's eye

and shrugged. There was no point in arguing, Wat had spoken.

The plasterer waded over to Giles. 'Thank your stars, you miserable sniveller, you puling schoolworm, that there's fellows here man enough to be women. Give me the gentlewoman's part and you, go and get one of your mates to swing on your ballocks till your voice drops if you want to be a man. All right, Adrian, let us proceed.'

'We'll take up where we left off last time. The Duke and Duchess are at the gate of Francisco's house with Valentine and Fabio and the gentlewoman.' Wat began rounding them up. 'Stephen, Francisco's wife comes to them in haste, *not* running.'

'How then?' Stephen said.

'Walk quickly. When you have your skirt on it will swinge about and make you seem hurried. Speak.'

'Good my lord Duke, my heart is glad to see
Yourself and gracious Duchess at our gate.
But where's Francisco? It was his intent
To ride a league to greet you on the way.
Met you not with him as you rode along?'

'Where's their horses, then?' Richard asked, predictably.

'Be quiet. Grooms have already led them away,' Wat said, over his shoulder.

'We saw him not,' Will said. 'Perchance he
    was delayed.'

'Not one hour since, he bid me stir and make
All ready for our guests, and then he went
With Honorius horseward,' Stephen said.

                                'Honorius is here?
Why has he left his fiefdom in the north?'

'He came last night, most pressing in his suit
To speak with my Francisco. Good Barnard!'

'That's you,' Wat said. 'Richard, get your arse on stage.'

'Barnard, hast thou yet seen thy noble lord?'

'He and his brother, Lord Honorius
Went to the stable where they talked awhile.
I have not seen him since. Honorius bides
Fast in his chamber,' Richard said.

                                'Let us to him then.
Mayhap Francisco with him we shall find.
They have not met in months and both must feel
Such parting sore, for since the cradle each
Has been as much a friend as brother to
The other. Daughter, be not so dismayed.
We will go in, and haply find the twain
Made four with friendship and with brotherhood.'

'What the hell does that mean?' Gilbert said. 'Made *four?*'

'If you imagine friendship and brotherhood as persons, with Honorius and Francisco that makes four,' Adam said.

'You need a tally-stick to follow this play,' Gilbert muttered.

The players were shuffling off, Wat in the rear with his hands up like paws, level with his shoulders.

'Give the dog a bone!' Jakey shouted.

'Hold your tongue. I'm bearing my lady's train.'

'I haven't got a train,' Henry said. 'Stop breathing down my neck, Wat.'

'Ah, but you will have a train and I'll be holding it up out of the muck. He will have a train, won't he?'

'Yes, he'll have a train,' Adrian said obediently. 'Now, all go out except Francisco's wife.'

Stephen remained alone on the stage, looking vacant.

'Pensive and distraught, Stephen,' Will said.

'What?'

'You must look pensive and distraught.'

'Where does it say that?'

'It doesn't say that, but can't you tell from your lines?

'I must look cheerly for the Duke my father,
But methinks brotherhood and friendship both
Bided at home when Honorius yesternight

169

Rode to our gate with choler at his heels
Like to a black dog.

Does that sound like someone who's about to break
into a jig?'

'The Duke isn't his – her – father, he's her husband's
father,' Richard said. 'Or has she married her brother?'

'Yes – no – the Duke's her husband's father but it's
proper for *her* to call him Father. He calls her Daughter.
If I put "in-law" every time, it would not scan.'

'Scan?'

'Save your questions for after, for God's sake,' Adrian
said. 'Stephen, get off, we'll do the scene where Honorius
meets the Duke and the Ghost appears.'

'I haven't said my lines, yet,' Stephen said.

'Will said them for you, near enough. Exit. Go on.
Next scene! A chamber in Francisco's house. Enter the
Duke with Fabio and Valentine. Enter Tobias.'

Everyone came back, followed by George
Wainwright.

'No, George, you don't come on behind them,' Adrian
said. 'Go round the other way and meet them.' George
set off in a wide circle. 'No, just come in from the other
side. Duke, begin.'

'Tobias, to your lord Honorius go
And bid him join us here, for we knew not

That he did bide in good Francisco's house.'
'Aye, my good lord.'

George scuttled off. Anthony, as Valentine, gazed after him.

'What ails the stammering knave?
His colour blanched like candle-light at dawn
When you did utter good Francisco's name.'

They might have been discussing someone who had failed to show up for a game of shove-groat at the Bear, but when Adam appeared as Honorius everyone put on their parts, for he wore his as comfortably as his coat.

'Enter the Ghost,' Adrian said. '*Matt*, that's you. Come on.'

Matt had put on the sheet, eager to do the thing properly. Entirely shrouded and unable to see where he was going he advanced crab-wise, cannoned into the Duke and veered off steeply.

'Matt, leave the sheet for now until you know where you have to walk. Remember, no one can see you.'

'Can't they?' Matt said. 'Why am I here, then?'

'I mean, only Honorius sees you.'

'What about the audience?'

'Yes, they see you, but in the play you appear only to Honorius, your murderer.'

'When did he murder me? I was never on before.'

'He murdered his brother, that's Hugh. You are the brother's ghost.'

'Am I?'

'Whose ghost did you think you were, for God's sake?'

'Oh, just one passing by, like the headless man in Swine Street,' Matt said. 'Now I understand.'

I doubt it, Adrian thought. There was a lot to be said for his father's suggestion that the ghost should never appear at all, except in the guilty sight of the murderer. 'Just say, "Honorius, dishonour'd Honorius", wait until Adam speaks to you and points, and go off again. Can you remember that?'

' 'tis a mouthful,' Matt complained. 'Honest dinosaurius. Exit,' he added cleverly.

They took it to the end of the scene, where Honorius, quaking and stuttering, declared his intention of returning to his home in the north. Fabio and Valentine were fallen into serious suspicion; Tobias and Barnard, once comrades in foolery, were now at each other's throats, and the Duke deeply perturbed. No sooner had Honorius left with Tobias behind him than Francisco's wife came staggering on, wringing her hands, to announce that her husband's body, its skull shattered, had been found in a ditch, wrapped in a bloody sheet, by his own faithful hound, while Jakey's bagpipe skirled its lamentation. For one miraculous moment Adrian believed what he saw, and as Will had predicted, the hair rose on the back of his neck, unfixed.

The yard of the Swan was twice the size of the one at the Bear, with galleries on three sides. Adrian and Will felt guilty about deserting the Bear but there was scarcely room in the yard there for the Morris to perform. And the choice was none of their doing. Once the council had approved the play Robert Croft had undertaken arrangements.

'If we erect the stage in the centre of the end gallery you can use the chamber behind it for a tiring room,' he said. 'There'll be curtains hung across to conceal the actors off-stage. Those who wish to pay extra to sit can line the galleries; the rest will stand in the yard as usual.'

'How wide will the stage be?' Will said.

'It's the one they put up for visiting companies, four yards by three. Master Jarvis says you may rehearse in the morning if you can get here by first light – and I think you ought. Your men are used to wandering about all over the churchyard – they had better find out in advance how it feels to be walking on solid boards – and to discover where the edge is. We don't want anyone falling off. How many more rehearsals have you?'

'Two,' Adrian said, 'not counting this last one on the morning of the play.'

'Enough, do you think?'

'Oh, yes.' He did not think it would be enough. If they rehearsed every evening between now and Whitsun it would not be enough; between now and Lammas, come to that, but if they failed it would not be for want of trying. He was cheered to think how devoted his company had become; if only their devotion were not so misplaced. Even now that they were able to run through the whole thing from start to finish he still had serious doubts about how much of it some of them understood. If only Will had stuck to the old Glovers' Play . . . but that was ungrateful. From an interlude with six characters, dealing with a story everyone knew by heart, he had woven this intricate tapestry of trust betrayed, brotherhood undone, an upright man driven to murder and exile. It was indeed heavy, but at least it would end on a merry note, with the dance to celebrate the birth of the Duke's son. Will was almost certain he could prevail upon his mother to loan them the infant Edmund. Which reminded him . . .

'Father, the pipe-and-tabor man.'

'Engaged; Jerome from Temple Grafton. And as Jakey will be otherwise occupied crying "Aye" and "Shame" with the rest of you that day, Jerome may play for the Morris as well.'

'That should make them look less like a funeral train than usual,' Will said. 'How do you know about "Aye" and "Shame"?'

'It's become a call around the town,' Robert said. 'People cry it at any excuse. For every man who says "Aye" another cries "Shame"! You may find they join in when they hear it spoken from the stage.'

'It won't be,' Adrian said, with relief. 'We cut it out.'

Eleven

Whit Sunday dawned cloudy and rain closed in by noon. Looking up at the tall windows during evensong Adrian saw the branches of the churchyard elms tossing and straining in the sudden wind, under their weight of wet leaves which tore loose and plastered themselves like scabs against the panes. When the service ended the congregation came out into a dank world of grey drizzle. The birds were enjoying it but the air was chill and the grass sodden underfoot. The wind had died down.

He glanced across at the green plot, trodden flat, where they had rehearsed during these last weeks. They would not tread there again. Tomorrow morning they would be treading boards in the yard of the Swan and tomorrow evening . . .

Will was a few paces ahead with his family. Adrian quickened his step.

'Do you realize, this time tomorrow we'll have done all we may. There will be nothing for it but to go before the town and let them see what we have made. When I heard the bellman in the market calling "Oyez!" and he announced the playing of *Fortune My Foe*, on Monday, after Whitsun, at four in the afternoon, I hardly understood that he was talking about *us*. What have we done?'

'This time tomorrow we'll find out. But look at it another way, if that frightens you. Whatever happens, time will run on. If it rains, if there is riot and pestilence, if a crazed boar runs wild through the Swan yard with an infant impaled on its tusks, if someone does fall off the stage – by Tuesday morning it will all be over.'

'What kind of a reputation will we have left to live with? What will men say when they see us go by? "There goes that fool Croft who thought he could run a company." '

' "There goes that fool Shakespeare who thought he could write a play." '

' "There goes a baker's dozen of fools who thought they could act." '

'No, leave out Adam, he *can* act. All goes better when he's on stage.'

'I'll be sorry to see him leave, when he moves on. I suppose he will move on.'

'Sure to. He has the summer ahead of him, and four more months of his antic humour to run.'

'I'll tell you who else can act,' Adrian said. 'Wat. We *were* fools not to see that sooner. He does not play the gentlewoman, he becomes her. He's taller than anyone else, shoulders like a weaver's beam, feet like cow pats, but when he comes on as the gentlewoman, no one laughs.'

'No one dares to.'

'True, but that's not why. He isn't funny. When he's the clown, Ralph, he's funny. When he plays the woman he's tender and gentle. We ought to have let him play the Duke – not that you aren't very good in it – or Honorius.'

'And then who'd play the gentlewoman? Could he have remembered so much?'

'I think he has the whole thing off by heart. Next time you write a play—'

'There'll be no next time. I hope to God no one laughs tomorrow evening – except in the fooling.'

'Amen to that,' Adrian said, 'and pray for clear skies while you're at it.'

They had arranged for the bellman to rouse them at four of the clock, but Will was awake long before sunrise and the sky was clear. A blessed calm milky light lay over the river mists as he leaned out of the upper window. Of the household, only Sir Solomon was up and about before him, strutting in the yard to rouse his sleepy womenfolk, but the elms were loud with early birdsong.

He kicked Gilbert awake, dressed and went downstairs,

swiping up bread and cheese left ready the night before, and crept into the shop to collect his hat.

The whole person of the Duke resided in the hat. Joan had done good work. Stitched into the crown all round was the long white wool, finely combed. At the sides she had contrived fleecy extensions, the thick strands swept forward and knotted, to rest under his nose, the ends teased out into full mustachios. It tickled, but it was better than a beard, which might work loose, and if a wind blew up it should keep the hat secured.

Gilbert came down and they went out by the back way, letting the latch fall softly, and slipped round the side of the house to where Adrian and Hugh were waiting for them in the street.

'Good morrow, Your Grace,' Hugh said, seeing the hat.

'Don't mock,' Will said. 'I never meant to play at all, remember. I thought writing the thing would be enough. If I'd known I was going to be the Duke I'd never have written the speeches so long. I didn't know what I was undertaking.'

'It's a good play, Will,' Adrian said. 'Everyone thinks so.'

'Everyone that's in it may think so. Today we find out what the town thinks.'

They walked down towards the Swan and as they went, others of the company fell in with them. By the time they were in sight of the inn the full fourteen were striding in step.

My Men, Adrian thought with pride. My company, our company. What had been two warring factions, the schoolboys and the workmen, were now united in common purpose. *I did that.*

'I feel lucky,' he said to Will. 'Do you feel lucky?'

'Wait till it's over,' Will said, but he was beginning to feel, if not lucky, at least confident. He had made this happen and they were all with him.

In the Swan yard the stage was up, the boards laid across hogsheads.

' 'tis passing small,' Richard said, doubtfully.

'It only looks so,' Hugh said, 'because we are accustomed to the churchyard. When you are up on it it will be as big as a room.'

'As big as a small room,' George said.

Adrian vaulted up and felt the solid resonant thud as he landed. The spectators' heads would be at about ankle height; the walls of the inn would contain the actors' voices and amplify them, the gallery above their heads serving as a sounding board. Beneath it hung curtains. As he was about to part them and look between, a head was thrust through from the other side. It belonged to Samuel Jarvis, the host of the Swan.

'Send your lads in round by the doorway, Adrian,' he

said. 'My wife will show them through. You come down this way.'

'Down?' Then he saw what the curtains concealed. Behind them was a window and the stage was slightly above the level of the broad sill. On the floor of the room Samuel had positioned a stout bench so that they could step up and down, to and from the stage.

'You can have this for a tiring room and come on and off straight through.' Samuel was an old hand at company productions. 'Here's all your costumes in the chest – best lay them out now.'

'I have a pipe-and-tabor man coming from Temple Grafton, and a bagpiper,' Adrian said. 'Can I station them above, in the gallery? They'll be out of the way of the players up there.'

'Bagpiper?' Samuel said. 'Not Jakey?'

'Jakey.'

'There's a lot to be said for going deaf,' Samuel remarked. The door opened and Will led the company into the tiring room. Samuel eyed them. 'I'll leave you to it, Adrian,' he said. 'Here's wishing you luck.'

Adrian gathered them round him and explained how they were to get out on to the stage. 'And if any man overturns that bench I'll do him a mortal hurt.'

'Best there's always two of us sitting on it,' Matt said. 'One each end to keep it steady.'

'Good idea. Now, the costumes were sent along last

night. Put them on and then everyone come out on stage.'

The stage seemed hopelessly inadequate when they were all standing on it. The four women in their skirts had expanded alarmingly. Henry's train was immediately whipped from his shoulders when somebody stepped on it.

'This won't do,' Matt said, teetering on the edge. 'We shall all be falling to our deaths.'

'No, you won't,' Adrian soothed him. He could comprehend the injured thatcher's fear. 'There's never a time when you're all on stage together except at the end when you come on and bow. This afternoon I'll be in the tiring room to direct you on and off, but for now I must stand out here in front to see what's going on, so I want no fooling there at the back. You must pay attention and *listen* so that you hear your cues. When you know that your part is coming step up on the bench so that you are ready to walk on. We're going to run straight through. I want all over and done with before people start wandering in off the street to watch. Save your questions till we're finished and we'll meet in the tiring room to answer them. Now, go off and wait for me to clap my hands and then Valentine walks on from the left—'

'My left or your left?' Anthony said.

'My left, the way you have always done it, nothing's

changed. You are reading a scroll – got the scroll? Then enter Fabio, right. Ready?'

He retreated to the middle of the yard while the company took themselves off. The stage lay before him, absurdly small and bare; they were all so accustomed to the spacious turf beneath their feet, the familiar stones of the church at their backs, the elms, the birds in the branches, water fowl on the river, the cuckoos calling in flight, and they were accustomed to playing to each other. What would happen when they were faced, for the first time, with an audience, hundreds of expectant faces staring up at them, waiting to be transported from the yard of the Swan in Bridge Street, Stratford, to the Ducal palace of Hungary, as Adam had described so long ago.

Well, as Will had said, ready or not, time would run on; he would find out what was going to happen soon enough and if things fell out badly at least it would all be over by sunset. He clapped his hands.

Anthony came through the curtains, treading gravely across the stage, head bent over his scroll. Giles appeared from the other side.

'How now, friend Valentine, tell me how things stand
Between the Duke and his two noble sons . . .'

Whether or not he had taken Wat's advice, his voice had dropped half an octave. Adrian stepped back a dozen paces, another six, he could still hear them.

'Where are you going?' Giles demanded.

'*Don't do that!*' Adrian yelled. 'I have to be sure you can be heard from all corners. Whatever I do, you keep going, understand? Tell the others, even if they can't see me, *keep going*. This must be finished in good time, otherwise we'll have half the town in here to see what's happening and it'll spoil the performance. And they won't have paid,' he added meaningly.

They kept going. Everyone knew his words, no one fell off the stage. The curtain came down only once when Richard tripped over it, revealing a row of open-mouthed faces, but at least he could see that they were following his instructions, listening and ready to walk on. The only thing that seemed to fall flat, to his surprise, was the fooling. George and Richard and Wat went through their paces, spoke their parts, executed intricate manoeuvres with the ladder, but it was all woefully unfunny. Still, he observed his own rule and said nothing, making a mental note to have a word with Wat afterwards, but what could he say? 'Wat, you just aren't funny'? Wat would knock him cold.

Adam was magnificent, the tortured hero falling from grace, embittered by his father's duplicity, betrayed by his brother, maddened to murder, finally fleeing, an anguished fugitive. Even the flatulent interventions of Jakey's bagpipe sounded appropriately dismal.

Had Will known what he was making when he took Cain and fashioned Honorius, like a weaver with a skein of plain white yarn creating a subtle-textured damask? More to the point, did he know *how* he had done it, could he do it again?

They were coming to the end, now. The Duke – and in spite of the white mustachios Will did not look a day over sixteen – stood with Fabio and Valentine lamenting the terrible outcome of his devious plan; one son dead, the other exiled; one wife a widow, the other abandoned. There was a moment's silence, two moments – what had happened? – then Wat burst through the curtains bearing a cushion aloft.

'Your Grace, prepare to arm yourself with joy.
The Duchess is delivered of a boy.'

'Put off all grief, this doleful night is run,
Salute the morn of our new-risen sun.'

This was supposed to be the cue for the pipe-and-tabor man who had not yet arrived. The dance was to be performed by six, Anthony, Giles and Adam, partnered by Gilbert, Stephen and Henry, out of character but still in their skirts and crowned with flowers – he must make sure the Butcher sisters had the wreaths ready in time. Jakey obliged on the bagpipe so that the gay galliard sounded like a Spanish pavanne. He was not at all sure what a galliard was supposed to sound like and nor, he suspected, was Will. He had simply liked the idea of it.

Adrian began to have doubts about the dance. Sure, they were all delighted by the arrival of the baby, but given what had gone before, would they be quite so ready to cast care aside? Perhaps Will could dash off an epilogue. But they had got through it and now the others were filing through the curtains to join them at the front of the stage, for the final bow. Would they be met this evening with clapping or rotten eggs?

Behind him a clatter of applause broke out. Samuel and his wife and two of the pot boys had gathered to watch the final scenes.

'What did you think?' Adrian said.

'A fine show. I don't understand above one word in five, mind you, but it was well done, for all that.'

Don't understand . . .? How could he tell Will?

'The echo, man.'

'I didn't hear the echo.'

'You didn't notice it. You know what all the words are, I dare say. But don't fret, there'll be no echo this evening with the yard full to bursting. Now, look to your company, they're all waiting to be told they played like angels. There's cakes and ale in the tiring room.'

Adrian waved to them to go in and got up on the stage to follow. The women were already divesting themselves with unwonted urgency.

'Take care!' Adrian called from the window sill. 'Fold those clothes and lay them neatly. You have to wear them again. Now look, Samuel has brought us refreshment. When you're ready let's sit down and I'll tell you what needs amending.'

'Hadn't you better tell them something else, first?' Adam said. 'They've sweated blood for you.'

'Oh, yes.' How graceless of him. 'It was well done,' he said, looking at them with pride. 'It was very well done.'

They settled round him.

'There's not much amiss. Now you have the feel of the boards beneath your feet you'll stop stamping, I've no doubt. That's you, Matt. A ghost should make no noise at all and you sound like an army coming on. Twice I heard a terrible crash – what was that?'

'The bench went over,' Hugh said. 'The first time, I sat down just as Wat stood up. The second time Richard and George sat down on the same end together and over it went.'

'We can't have that,' Adrian said. 'I know it was not done on purpose, but the audience will think it is meant for Jove's thunderbolts or the roof falling in.'

'Best we move this great table over and enter from that,' Adam said. 'More room and we can't upset it.'

'Good thinking. See to it. Likewise, some of you are talking – all that can be heard at the front. Don't look innocent, I know who it was by the voices, and make sure that you are standing upright before you part the curtains. Fabio came out once on all fours. Wat, remember, when you come on at the end this evening you'll have a live baby, Will's little brother. Babies have a top and a bottom. Unless you want Mistress Shakespeare to come after you with a skillet, make sure you have him right side up. You don't wave him in the air as you did with the cushion. He's not a month old yet, and tender.'

'As if I would.' Wat bridled with mock indignation. 'Go on.'

Adrian hesitated.

'There's something else you wanted to say, wasn't there?'

'Yes. Hugh—'

'No, not to Hugh, to me – me and George and Richard. Don't be afeared.'

Adrian looked him in the eye. 'What went wrong?'

Wat roared. 'What did you think I'd do, take offence and smite you?' He looked around. 'You know what he wants to say, don't you? Why weren't we funny? And we weren't. Were you laughing back here?'

Tentatively heads were shaken.

'No, you weren't, and nor was Adrian. And do you know why? Because we couldn't see you. When we do our fooling we need to see you and hear you laugh, like you did in the churchyard. Why, then we fool the more. It'll be all right this evening, Adrian, be sure. When we have our audience, we'll be funny.'

'Thanks, Wat,' Adrian said, with real gratitude. How was it that rude unlettered Wat understood so much that the others did not?

'And the rest of 'em will be the more tragical, you'll see. What did you want to say to Hugh?'

'I can't remember, it couldn't have been much. Now, go your ways and we'll all meet here this afternoon at three, to start at four. And, no one is to get drunk beforehand. I know it's a holiday but people are looking to us to be the crown of it. Stay sober.'

Twelve

They stood in the tiring room listening to the swelling growl of the audience assembling in the yard. Adrian had been part of such a crowd often enough, an atomy of the good nature and excitement, yelling along with everyone else to make himself heard. Now he detected a previously unnoticed menace in the sound of hundreds massed against him, him and his company.

He stepped up on to the table and put his eye to the gap between the curtains. As far as he could see, the yard was paved with heads, the noise seemed to stir the fabric like wind in a sail. He felt palpable terror at his back, the room vibrated with it. At some point everyone had been to the curtain, first to see if they would get an audience at all, then to estimate the numbers, and finally to quake at the size of it. The whole town must be out there; the side galleries were packed; Dad was sitting with Giles Butcher's father . . . Henry's parents . . . there were the Shakespeares. Dick was laying about him with a bladder on a stick, but by God the old man looked grim, waiting for Will and Gilbert to make a spectacle of

190

themselves. They were all going to bring down shame upon their families . . . Dad had *trusted* him . . . and the council . . . nine and sevenpence . . .

'Is it time?' Will gazed up at him, face whiter than his whiskers.

'Samuel will give the signal, he's standing at the gate,' Adam said. Adam at least was calm. 'When the yard's full he'll make a sign to Jerome, who'll give a flourish. Adrian, you step out as soon as you hear him. They'll see you mean to speak and fall silent.'

'You do it,' Adrian begged. 'They won't fall silent for me.'

'Yes they will, and they'll applaud when you've spoken, and that will give you heart. It will give us all heart.'

Adrian looked down at his company. They were all, even Wat, stricken dumb at the thought of what lay on the far side of the curtains. They needed heart. It was his duty to give it to them.

He took a squint at the yard again and his bowels melted. This mob was never going to fall silent for him. He had on his best doublet and a clean collar, his cap adorned with a glistening feather from Sir Solomon's tail, that Joan had given him, but he was not in costume, he had no false whiskers to hide behind.

And what the devil was he to say? My lords, ladies and gentlemen . . . and women? Gentlewomen? What

was the damned play called now? *Two Noble Kinsmen* –
no – oh God—

Up above, he knew, Jerome was waiting with the
Guildhall trumpet. Then he saw Samuel at the back of
the crowd, in the gateway, waving a cloth on a pole. The
brazen whoop of the flourish made him start, but
the noise outside seemed to subside a little, faces were
turning towards the stage, towards *him*. Someone poked
him in the back. He parted the curtains and stepped out.

A miracle! Hush fell, although the silence of hundreds
was not silent. He still did not know what he would say,
but his feet carried him to the front of the stage.

'My lords, ladies, gentles all, today our company
will play *Fortune My Foe*, a tragedy, by William
Shakespeare.'

Another miracle: as Adam had predicted, applause
broke out. He thought he heard laughter, too, but it was
all good-humoured. He bowed, stepped back and ducked
through the curtains.

'You're on, Anthony. Here's good luck to you. Good
luck to you all.'

'Don't tempt Fate!' Adam cried.

'Well, may you all break your legs, then,' Adrian said,
as Anthony pushed past him and strode on to the stage.
On his other side, Giles followed.

' "How now, friend Valentine . . ." ' and they were off.

★　★　★

The Duke and Duchess advanced to the front and stood together, clasping hands.

> 'Madam, behold you where the moon's great orb,
> Like a pale mirror to the sun's fair face,
> Hangs in the east . . .'

A voice called out, 'Nay, 'tis the sun!'

Unfortunately, it was, exactly where Will was pointing, above the inn's chimney. Wat's argument came back to him; why hadn't he thought of that?

> '. . . and smiles upon our joy.'

'As doth the moon wax great then so shall I,' Henry said. Will gazed tenderly into his face. He had learned to ignore the squint.

> 'For as it is with women, so with me;
> There beats a second heart within this breast.
> And may kind Fortune bless us with a boy,
> A worthy brother to Your Grace's sons.'

The voice rang out again. 'In God's name, this is not Hungary but that very isle in the Sea of Ocean where the women have men's parts and the men bear children!'

Someone else had been reading Sir John Mandeville.

'Pay them no heed,' Will muttered to Henry who halted and stumbled over his next speech. They played to the end of the scene; the interruptions had been met with a few coarse guffaws but with more indignant hisses for silence. Will thought he recognized the voices but he could not stare directly at the place they were coming from. The side galleries were packed, he had already noticed his father and mother sitting with Dick, on the left, and there was Philip, generously present to watch what he could not share. And there, at his feet, was Katherine Page, with the journeyman from the woollendraper's gnawing her neck. He hoped Adrian had not seen them. Whoever was calling out sat on the right-hand gallery, close to the corner. As he led Henry towards the curtain he risked a side-long glance from under his white hairs and hat, in that direction. The glance was noted.

'Take care, Duchess, of that wolf in sheep's clothing! Baaaaah!'

'That's no wolf! 'tis but a whelp yet.'

'Say, lady, does he take off that hat in bed, and his wool with it?

More bleats followed him off-stage, directed at his mustachios, no doubt. He *knew* those voices, but he had not seen the faces clearly, they appeared to be enveloped in vapour. A curious odour emanated from that corner, a kind of burning, like leaves, rather as he had always imagined frankincense to smell.

In the tiring room he whipped off the hat and cloak and headed for the door.

'Where are you going?' Adrian grabbed his arm.

'I'm off-stage for a good ten minutes. Don't you hear the heckling? I know where it's coming from.'

'It's only some fools. Nobody marks them.'

'It's more than that, and they've got some kind of a fire going. It could be dangerous. I can't do anything, but Samuel ought to know.'

On stage Valentine was divulging to Fabio the Duke's true purpose in giving over the cares of the country to his sons. Will slipped outside, sprinted up the stairs and out on to the gallery where Jakey and Jerome from Temple Grafton were leaning over the balustrade, watching the proceedings below. The view was severely foreshortened but they seemed to be enjoying themselves.

He could not walk upright for fear of distracting the audience who might think his presence there was part of the action. Instead he went down on hands and knees and crawled behind the gallery rail. Jakey saw him coming without surprise. Anything might happen in a play, he had learned.

'It goes well,' he remarked. 'Jerome here is watching it.' Jerome nodded. Will was gratified to see that he was following the action intently. 'Me, I'm watching the people,' Jakey said. 'It's a rare sight to see so many pleased by what we do.'

'Have you been watching that cloud of smoke in the corner?' Will pointed along the gallery. 'What's going on?'

'Happen they're cooking their supper,' Jakey said tolerantly.

Will crawled past them to the end of the gallery and raised his head cautiously. At right angles to him sat Peter Starling, his man Capon and two other young bloods, wielding what looked to be musical instruments, long white reeds of clay with little bowls on the ends. The fire was in the bowls, they put the reeds in their mouths and sucked. The bowls glowed red and out of their noses came smoke. This must be the herb tobacco. Men smoked it for enjoyment, he'd heard, but he was prepared to wager that they had brought along their pipes to cause a diversion, along with their verbal interpolations.

He wanted to climb over and smash their faces in, and their pipes; let them swallow their foul weed and choke. Did they seek only to annoy or did they hope that someone would shout 'Fire!' and start a panic? People could be killed in the press to escape. Was there no law against smoking tobacco pipes in a public place?

There was nothing he could do that might not start

196

an altercation. Asking them politely to desist would have the opposite effect. If he allowed them to goad him he would let fly with his fists. Even at one against four he could do a lot of damage, but it would count as starting an affray, and he would be the one who ended up in the stocks, accused of assaulting gentlemen. Gentle! He could only pray that the company would rise above the insults and play on – which reminded him that the scene below was almost played out; he must go down, put on his hat and mustachios and be the Duke again.

At ground level he ran into Wat who was lounging in the doorway with his ladder.

'Been to put out the fire?' he inquired. 'My ladder would have been a quicker way.'

'It's not a fire, Wat, they're smoking tobacco.'

'It smells like a fire, in a turnip clamp,' Wat said.

'It's on purpose to spoil our play, I'll warrant you.'

'Have you met them before? Do you know their names?' Wat said, casually.

'I've met them before; Peter Starling and his man Capon.'

Wat's smile underwent an ungodly transfiguration. 'Capon and Starling? Oh, a gift, a gift . . .'

Will raced indoors, clutched up the hat and sprang on to the stage in time for Francisco, now apprised of his father's plan, to speak poison in his ear against Honorius. When Honorius came to bid the Duke farewell he was received coolly and sent on his way coldly. The audience booed and hissed with relish, but the boos were mixed with bleats, and Will heard nothing else.

Honorius and Francisco prepared to leave the Duke's palace, one bound for the north, the other for the south. Their servants, Tobias and Barnard, were packing for the journeys. As they came out on stage they carried a large wicker basket between them. Adrian watched nervously. It was their entrance that had brought down the curtains this morning.

'Where's Wat? He's supposed to follow them on.'

'Ah, he had a sudden good idea,' Adam said. 'He's coming in through the crowd.'

'Why? I wish he wouldn't do things like this.'

'The ladder. He pushes his way through, sets up the ladder and climbs on to the stage.'

'It's meant to be a stable yard.'

'No one will mind about that. Here he comes.'

A huge wave of laughter announced that Wat was approaching. The ladder clove a path through the standing spectators and Adrian saw his grin appear above the edge of the stage. He pulled up the ladder behind him, hoisting it across his shoulder, caught first Richard, then George, with the ends of it, and they swung into their routine. The laughter became continuous. The ladder was set up against the gallery, Richard climbed it and fell off. Wat knocked it down and caught George's head between the rungs. They set it across the basket and sat down, George on one end, Wat on the other, seesawing. Wat stood up, George fell off.

'That's new, too.'

'It's what happened this morning, with the bench.'

Wat began to extemporize. 'I do hear that in England there be men who breath fire and smoke, like the dragons of old time.'

'What, out of their noses?' Richard said, catching on.

'Nay, out of their arses, right fiery farts,' Wat said. 'But when there are ladies present they do put pipes in their mouths to draw out the sparks more seemly.'

The audience also caught on and hands began pointing at the right-hand corner of the gallery.

'What are you pointing at?' Wat demanded. 'There's nothing up there but birds, capons and starlings, one fit for the table and the other fit for nothing.' He leaned the ladder against the gallery and swarmed up it for a closer look. Starling and his party saw him coming and prudently withdrew.

'Vanished in a puff of smoke,' Wat observed, descending.

'They'll make us pay for that,' Will said.

'Afterwards, perhaps. They dare do nothing now.'

'It's afterwards I'm worried about. We're only halfway through.'

The fooling ended with Richard and George putting the ladder away. While their backs were turned Wat climbed into the basket.

'That ladder was my way in to the palace,' he remarked, closing the lid, 'and this is my way out.' As Richard and George struggled to carry the basket off-stage he raised the lid and waved farewell, to riotous applause from the yard and, no doubt, a signal lack of it from the corner of the gallery.

Things became serious again immediately. Francisco, at home with his wife, received a visit from Honorius. They quarrelled, Honorius slew Francisco and concealed his body with the help of Tobias. The Duke arrived and asked to see Francisco; Honorius denied all knowledge of his brother's whereabouts. It was the cue for Matt's first entrance.

Mindful of his footfalls he had removed his shoes and glided on-stage shrouded in the bloody sheet. They had adjusted the knot at the top to compensate for the angle of Matt's head and slit eyeholes in the bloodstains. The gallery woke up again. A shrill squeal broke out.

'Eeeeeeeh! A phantom! Murder and walking spirits!'

Matt's head emerged from the sheet. 'Nay, peace, be not afeared,' he said. 'I am no spirit. I am Matthew Ibbetson the thatcher.' He rearranged the sheet. 'Dishonest anorius,' he intoned.

'Goddamit!' Adrian swore. In spite of themselves the crowd had laughed, the effect was ruined. He could see Will centre-stage, losing his temper; if he lost all control of it he might undo them all. Now they were being paid back for Wat's fooling. Damn them for gentlemen, their conduct was not gentle, but none here dare touch them. The company could do nothing but endure the barracking from their betters.

But the crowd thought differently. As the lady-like shriek rose again at Matt's second appearance they began to growl threateningly, safe in the knowledge that they were collectively faceless plebians. Some had brought along rotten vegetables in case the play displeased them. Having positioned themselves conveniently near the front they were well-placed to lob a few towards the gallery. No one moved to intervene. The constables stayed well back. The third time Francisco's ghost walked, there were no screams.

A few minutes before the end Samuel's wife tiptoed into the tiring room followed by Joan bearing the infant Edmund. Wat, now kirtled-up again as the gentlewoman, advanced bear-like to receive him. Joan's eyes widened in alarm. What hairy nurse was this?

'Don't worry, darling, I'm to carry him on,' Wat whispered, 'and I'll handle him as tenderly as any suckling pig.' His huge hands closed around the sleeping baby. 'Wake up, lambkin, you're supposed to wave.'

'Get on *now*,' Adrian said, plucking his sleeve.

'Is my wimple straight?' Wat said.

'Yes. Yes, get *on*.' He held back the curtain and Wat sailed out.

> 'Your Grace, prepare to arm yourself with joy,
> The Duchess is delivered of a boy.'

He raised Edmund aloft as though he were indeed serving a piglet at dinner. Will grabbed his brother and hurriedly hugged him close before he could start screaming. Then he faced the audience for the last time.

> 'Put off all grief, this doleful night is run.
> Salute the morn of our new-risen sun.'

He stepped back, aware of delighted cooing from the crowd; this was their master stroke, a real live baby. As he turned to leave the stage Edmund woke up in time to grip hold of the mustachios. The Duke's facial hair came away in a fistful, leaving him clean-shaven. Jerome struck up on his pipe and tabor, the dancers came out and he slipped back between the curtains where Joan was waiting anxiously.

'He's leaking. Take him to Mother.'

'We'll make an actor of you yet, chuck,' Wat crooned.

On stage the dance was ending. Adrian marshalled his

company and ushered them out through the curtains. 'Go on, Will.'

'And you,' Will said. They linked arms and followed the others, lining up at the front of the stage to bow acknowledgement of the applause. It was an enormous sound, hundreds of clapping hands, voices cheering, calling out names of their favourite players; sons, brothers and sweethearts. Most voices were raised for Wat, but Adrian saw only Katherine fling off the woollendraper's journeyman with an Amazonian shrug and hold out her arms to him.

And why wouldn't they applaud us? he thought, bowing and bowing again. We gave them a good time; that's what they came for and we saw they got it. There was no sound from the corner of the gallery. Whoever had sat there had left discreetly. A deliquescent cabbage dripped from the eaves.

Beside him Will was bowing in time with the others. He thought, they liked the play, but they don't care who wrote it. They've probably forgotten it was me. But they liked it. It played well. It was not bad for a first effort — no, it was *good*. We didn't disgrace ourselves.

Even Father was pleased, standing up to acknowledge his eldest sons, with Mother beside him and Dick, waving a bladder on a stick. That old glover of the north country would never have recognized his play, but without it they would not be standing here now, cheered and applauded. In a way, as he had hoped, they had made it live on after him, and Father, Will knew, was thanking him for it. Father, of course, had never read it.

Beneath the uproar he heard a still small voice. '*They* think you've done well, but you know better. It was not well done, parts of it were passing shameful. If it hadn't been for Adam we'd have been laughed off the stage in places. If it hadn't been for Wat, the fooling would have fallen flat. Next time, remember how . . .'

Next time? He had never thought of writing another play. He had done what he set out to do, given the town its Whitsun pastime, and now it was over. Tomorrow he'd be back in the glove shop, learning his trade; but the happy faces of his company, his comrades, lightened his heart, and the applause was sweet to his ears.